The Yukon in
PERIL

A Sherlock Holmes Mystery Adventure

R McIntyre Cooke

To order additional copies of this book, contact:
Bookwhip
1-855-339-3589
https://www.bookwhip.com

In memory of Frederick, who loved his country. The author would like to thank Carolyn for master document know-how; thanks also to Jeff for lending his artistic skills; and certainly thanks to Connie for too much to recite.

Let us take a patriot, where we can meet him; and, that we may not flatter ourselves by false appearances, distinguish those marks that are certain from those that may deceive; for a man may have the external appearance of a patriot, without constituent qualities; as false coins have often lustre, though they want weight.

—Dr Samuel Johnson

PREFACE

It was the intention of Mr Holmes that the details relative to the proffered knighthood, which he turned down some time ago, should not be disclosed to the public. In the interest of the historical record, however, I have taken it upon myself to preserve an account of these events in the belief that someday a grateful public will be apprised of the unique contribution my dear friend made in the interest of this island nation, whose glorious sovereign perceived him worthy of a baronetcy, but for whom discretion and the suasion of the Foreign Office dictated no public recognition. I suggest that the reader of this document, whomever it may be, and at whatever future date, should carefully evaluate the following account and judge for himself the perilous nature of these events, the sterling manner in which Mr Sherlock Holmes of 221B Baker Street coped with them, and the immeasurable contribution that he thereby made to Her Majesty's Government and to the entire British people. At such a time, with careful consideration, the reader may then determine the appropriateness of its further circulation or even its publication.[1]

John H Watson, MD

---

[1] Vincent Starrett questions the oftrepeated claim by Watson of Holmes' modesty, asserting that the latter was not averse to publicity. The numerous allusions to untold tales, Starrett is inclined to attribute to a certain indolence and disinclination on the doctor's part. See Vincent Starrett, *The Private Life of Sherlock Holmes* (New York: Pinnacle Books, 1975), 101 ff [previously republished by University of Chicago Press, 1960, enlarged by the author from the original 1933 edition].The present document reveals the selfless patriotism of both men.

BAKER STREET

Sherlock Holmes and I had just consumed a rather substantial breakfast, complete with soft-boiled eggs, a rasher of bacon, and Mrs Hudson's marmalade on hot buttered toast. The mid-March morning showed some signs of respite from the rains that had persisted for the best part of a fortnight. Masculine footfalls upon the stairway attested to the fact that we were about to have an early morning visitor. Mrs Hudson's slightly petulant directions to the visitor, as they faintly reached our ears, suggested that our caller had been hasty to the point of curtness. In a moment, a sharp rap shook the door.

There stood a young man of perhaps thirty-eight years, dressed in a proper but nondescript manner. I glanced at my pocket watch and took note of the time—five and twenty past nine. Our caller was obviously not on his own time. The rapid ascent of the stair suggested urgency, and he was quite out of breath.

"Mr Holmes?" he queried, looking directly at my colleague. (I recall wondering with a faint sense of annoyance, I confess, why Holmes' identity was so obvious, as we stood side-by-side.)

Holmes nodded crisply, muttering an acknowledgment and awaiting the stranger's own offer of identification.

"My name is Hadley Habakkuk," the man continued. There was a hint of arrogance in his tone, and clearly Holmes was convinced already that the rather gaunt figure before us had little reason for superior airs.

"Ah, Habakkuk, is it? Yes. And this is my colleague, Dr Watson."

I had expected Holmes would offer Habakkuk a cup of coffee since a freshly brewed pot sat invitingly on the table where Mrs Hudson had placed it a few minutes before. But it was obvious that my friend had no intention of abetting the man's apparent haughtiness. Instead, Holmes studied him with more curiosity than deference.

"I see you are a clerk at the Colonial Office," Holmes observed.

"Quite," our visitor responded, with more than a hint of surprise in his voice. The monocle that he had been twisting rapidly between thumb and forefinger, he now affixed to his right eye. There it hung perilously as he tilted his head inquiringly to the side, evidently developing an instantaneous increase in the respect with which he viewed the lean detective. Holmes returned his gaze with what I took to be mild amusement.

"And what is the nature of your business with me?" Holmes broke the silence. The atmosphere was not very congenial.

"As you astutely concluded, I do represent the Colonial Office, though not entirely in an official capacity—at least not yet. My superior has asked me to contract you discreetly concerning a matter of some importance, to determine your willingness to be of assistance to Her Majesty's Government. Indeed, I am authorized to tell you that the Colonial Secretary himself has mentioned your name in the highest circles, regarding the affair at hand."

"I beg you, young fellow, to speak less obliquely." It was clear that Holmes now had the upper hand.

A matter of some importance to Her Majesty's Government, I thought, and how would Holmes react to such an inauspicious initial contact? I recalled the anger that Mr Mycroft Holmes had engendered in his younger brother when, on more than one occasion, he had drawn my friend into certain clandestine matters, ostensibly on behalf of our beloved nation. Few of those who have followed my earlier accounts are likely to have thought much about the world's greatest consulting detective in terms of his patriotic zeal or even his political inclinations. But let me assure one and all that my good friend is not lacking in either noble sentiment concerning the land of his birth or solid grasp of political principles and partisan issues of the day.

The appearance of our bony visitor reminded me of that desperate chap, Percy Phelps, who, a decade back, had approached my colleague in such agitation over the purloined naval treaty–the secret treaty between Britain and Italy. Then, Holmes's services had saved our nation potentially serious embarrassment.[2]

Indicating the empty chair by the sideboard to Habakkuk, Holmes returned to his own chair by the littered breakfast table. I could see that, for the moment at least, he would hear out the now discomfited clerk. Faintly amused and not a little curious, I sat down myself.

"These are difficult times for us and for the Foreign Office. The present unpleasantness with the Boers ... and ... and .... And the Venezuelan boundary matter has not been conducive to the best relations with the Americans, you know. And, of course, the Kaiser has been, well, not only unpredictable but downright—"[3]

"Yes, yes," Holmes injected impatiently. "There are those who enjoy twisting the lion's tail, and this is not at all surprising when one considers that Great Britain occupies such a paramount position in the world today. Less happy lands must feel a tinge of envy."

Rarely had my friend so openly expressed his sentiments. "I plead your indulgence, Mr Holmes. I had no intention of lecturing you on contemporary affairs. Your reputation for forthrightness and incisiveness does not do you full justice. Clearly, you are cognizant of these matters far more fully than your humble servant," Habakkuk conceded, in what now appeared to be near obsequiousness.

I felt a bit sorry for the fellow. My original distaste had vanished as the clerk before me so rapidly lost his affectations. His quite ordinary appearance, which had been somewhat disguised by his initial haughtiness, now stood exposed fully in the unrelenting greys of his greatcoat, spindly trouser legs, and spats. His monocle hung forlornly on his right lapel.

"Habakkuk," I interjected, "Mr Holmes has as much affection for queen and country as any of Her Britannic Majesty's loyal subjects. And

---

2   "The Naval Treaty," *The Strand Magazine*, October and November 1893.

3   Evidently a reference to the Kruger telegram: Kaiser Wilhelm to Paul Kruger, January 1896, congratulating him on his success against the British. The telegram added tension to Anglo-German relations.

I might add, I share entirely his sentiments. One does not serve with the Fifth Northumberland Fusiliers in the heat and peril of India without developing a most healthy attachment to our noble land."

"Well said, Watson, but our early morning guest has not come to hear an affirmation of our chauvinistic sentiments. And anyway, as Dr Johnson was wont to remind us, patriotism is the last refuge of a scoundrel."

Our visitor now seemed anxious to conclude his business.

"Would you …. Could you agree to meet with one who, I assure you, is identified with the highest echelons of the present Government? And I mean the highest!" he emphasized.

With that, the clerk thrust a sealed note into Holmes's hand. Habakkuk stepped towards the door as Holmes broke the seal and unfolded the single sheet. I had the temerity to glance at it as he perused its brief contents. If I am not mistaken, it read as follows:

Dear Mr Holmes,

This note will confirm the authority of the bearer to arrange a meeting at your earliest convenience. The PM and I agree. You are our man.

J. C.

Holmes studied our early morning guest thoughtfully for a moment.

"Yes," he nodded crisply. Clearly he was assessing the import of this last revelation. The Colonial Secretary, and likely even the Prime Minister himself, were were privy to this informal but apparently urgent contact.

"If it would be convenient, Mr Holmes, call at the Travellers at two o'clock today. That was his suggestion. He will be most grateful for your positive response. But please regard this matter as confidential and unofficial—at least for the moment. Thank you, sir, thank you."

Habakkuk opened the door, buttoning his greatcoat as he backed into the hallway. With a tip of his hat, he turned and descended the stairs in what I took to be grateful retreat. The street door closed quickly. A squeak in the lower hall floor suggested that Mrs Hudson was watching the gentleman cross the sidewalk and retrace his course towards Whitehall. The sun was now illuminating brightly the Axminster rug where Holmes stood, apparently musing about the events of the past few minutes.

"How the devil did you know our caller was from the Colonial Office, Holmes?" I asked.

"Clearly a civil servant, obvious to even the casual observer. At his age, unlikely to use a monocle except as a rather youthful affectation. And who but Joe Chamberlain is more noted for such an optical aid? So it seemed a reasonable guess that our young sycophant was consciously or unconsciously emulating the Colonial Secretary himself."

"Quite right, Holmes, quite right. But really then, mostly a lucky guess."

"An educated guess, yes. Perhaps luck is something one makes for himself."

Mrs Hudson could be heard climbing the stairs. She would want to clear the breakfast dishes. As she entered the room, Holmes seemed oblivious to her. The good woman nodded briefly to me and glanced quizzically at Holmes, who now faced the window contemplating the bright shafts of sunlight that penetrated Baker Street. Gathering cups, plates, and marmalade jar onto her tray, she cleared her throat, as if to offer an observation either on the mess we had left, the full pot of untouched coffee, or else upon the disagreeable demeanour of our recent visitor. Apparently thinking the better of it, however, she withdrew without a word.

"Surely the public school did not infect Habakkuk with those unpleasant airs," I observed, a bit sarcastically I confess.

"A public school education may teach one not to be lewd, but it doesn't guarantee that one will be pleasant," Holmes laughed.

Holmes tossed his maroon smoking jacket aside as if suddenly making a clear decision.

"The Travellers," he mused, "tends to be the haunts of the Foreign Office, with a coffee room jammed with supercilious second secretaries. The food is reputed to be rather bad."

THE TRAVELLERS

Ah, well," said Holmes as we approached the Travellers, "we shall soon see what's afoot, Watson."

The doorman officiously admitted us, after assuring himself of our identity. "Indeed, you are expected," he intoned. "There, to the stairs and then to your right, gentlemen."

The iron duke's visage peered down on us everywhere. "It was Wellington's support that brought this club into existence, Watson. We cannot begrudge him a prominent place in it," Holmes confided quietly as we gained the second floor. Conversation was virtually forbidden; even the muffled sound of our footfalls seemed to reverberate intrusively.

"This handrail was installed for Talleyrand's benefit," Holmes reflected.

"Really," I replied, "I hope the politicians we are about to deal with are less chameleon than he."

From a shadowy alcove, a figure beckoned. Holmes and I approached with—for myself at least—considerable curiosity. I may have emitted a bit of a gasp, as the great glistening forehead and ample beard became clear. There stood the marquis himself. For nearly the past twenty years, he had virtually dominated the politics of our land. And now, with a firm handshake and a gesture towards the settee and chairs by the wall, he bid us sit down. My initial impression was that we were in the presence of an authentic grandee, despite his ill-fitting attire.

"The need for privacy and the utmost discretion led me to arrange this meeting here. Downing Street is too public, and I think we can count on this rendezvous remaining totally confidential. These are not my usual haunts, but a close confidant kindly has arranged that we shall be undisturbed."

The Prime Minister spoke with quiet intensity.

"But excuse me," he said, breaking his line of thought, "I must thank you for coming when you were left so uninformed about the business at hand. May I also apologize for the clerk from the Colonial Office? What he lacks in position and decorum, he makes up for in anonymity. It is not likely that anyone is watching his whereabouts very closely. That is why Joe and I sent him your way."

The marquis paused and again invited us to be seated. I felt quite awestruck. Holmes seemed entirely at ease and only waited for our host to move towards a seat before he did likewise.

"Do you know my associate, Dr Watson, Prime Minister?"

"Only by reputation, Mr Holmes. I am indeed aware of his past collaboration with you, and it is a pleasure to make your acquaintance, doctor."

"Your servant, sir," I replied.

"We thought it best that only one of us meet you here. The Colonial Secretary sends his regards and thanks you for your prompt response to his note. Mr Mycroft Holmes assured him of your willingness and ability to be of service in the matter at hand. For myself, I am satisfied that his confidence is well placed, and I chose to meet you personally, so that the importance Her Majesty's Government places upon this will be fully apparent."

The marquis again paused and looked at each of us intently. Clearly, he was a leader of men.

"If today's proceeding are a bit unorthodox, the reasons behind them will, I trust, soon be clear."

Holmes simply nodded, anxious to hear more.

With a slight sigh, our host glanced beyond our alcove to the cavernous room and hallway beyond. Total silence prevailed for a moment. The Prime Minister leaned forward with earnestness and proceeded to confide in us with measured words.

"These are not easy days to serve in the Premiership, and occasionally the added burden of the Foreign Office seems a task beyond human capacity.[4] Britain's global commitments seem to compound the difficulties of our policies at home and abroad. A great and glorious empire calls for vigilance and ingenuity in crafting our diplomatic stances. And now, while we face the prospect of an inglorious conflict in South Africa, boundary disputes in South America—and God knows where else—another difficulty has presented itself in a most unlikely place. I refer to the Canadian north, to wit, the Yukon—more specifically, the Klondike."

Holmes and I nodded. For the past year or two, news of the Klondike gold rush had been widely publicized in the press, particularly the cheaper dailies.

"You are undoubtedly aware of the fact that the Americans are making a claim concerning the Yukon-Alaska boundary that is quite at odds with the interpretation that our Canadian brethren have asserted. At stake, among other things, is possession of the port of Skagway—and I employ the term *port* loosely. As modest a collection of shanties and piers as Skagway may be, geography and topography dictate that it has become the major entrepôt for the bulk of the manpower and materiel that have poured, and continue to pour, into the Yukon. Like it or not, that territory is being inundated with a deluge of humankind such as has become all too familiar in the gold rushes of our century."

I hung on the marquis's every word, though not grasping the purpose of his recital.

"Now, we are not unaware of the course of events that frequently develop in these circumstances. The Spanish in California soon learned the consequences of the massive influx of English-speaking Americans in the rush of 1849. Our own imperial resources were tested to the maximum by the intrusion of thousands of American fortune seekers in the Caribou rush of a few years later. And now the Yukon."

---

[4]   In 1900, Salisbury relinquished the Foreign Office and became Lord Privy Seal.

There was an ominous note in his last words. Leaning forward still further, his voice dropped to a whisper.

"Only last month, the Boundary Commission that has been endeavouring to resolve the issues that separate us has been adjourned until midsummer, and I would not be surprised if it is not reconvened. President McKinley's moderation has provoked noisy protests in the American Pacific Northwest. And the Canadians have shown no greater inclination to be accommodating. I understand Laurier–that frog premier–has stated he will not allow the Americans to intimidate or bamboozle him. So diplomatically, you see, we approach an awkward impasse. We surely have no desire to alienate the republic at this time, but we must, of course, give the Canadians no reason to doubt our firm backing. Such are the burdens of office. Such are the burdens of charting a noble course for a great nation."

The PM sighed. He did not look happy.

"The last thing Her Majesty's Government wants now is new difficulty with the Americans. Indeed, we would most warmly welcome a new era of good will with our republican cousins. The times seem right. Englishmen in the streets are enthusiastic for America's little war with Spain. Chamberlain has made known our sympathies. And the truth of the matter is–we need friends! Our diplomatic stance has left us without allies. Despite what is often said of me, I find nothing splendid in isolation at all."

I felt a rush of sympathy for the noble statesman before us.

"You must understand, gentlemen, Her Majesty's Government must balance carefully a policy of comity with America and our commitments to the senior Dominion within the British Empire."

"Yes, Your Lordship," Holmes injected. "You have apprised us most skilfully, and with an economy of words, of the present situation. But, if I may be so bold, may I enquire where my colleague and I fit into your considerations."

That was Holmes for you. Even in the august presence of so notable an aristocrat, he was impatient to get to the heart of the matter. Salisbury drew a handkerchief from his pocket and wiped his enormous brow and then dabbed his ample white moustache. His luxuriant white beard glistened in a beam of mid-afternoon sunlight that momentarily broke through the clouds that had gathered since the promising break in the weather this morning. Fortunately, the marquis did not seem to have taken any offense at Holmes's gentle but impatient prodding. At any rate, he resumed his discourse with no sign of irritation.

"Alas, this is where a most difficult problem emerges. And this is where you can assist us. Word comes to me by way of the Home Secretary that there are those within these isles who plan to make mischief for Her Majesty's Government in this very connection. The Special Crimes Division, whose assignment it is to keep an eye on the vast and growing variety of radicals, anarchists, and nihilists of foreign and domestic origin who infest our land, has conveyed some disturbing news. God save us from ourselves! For years, this country has given shelter to every kind of malcontent, misguided idealist, political misfit, and miscreant imaginable. Fortunately they have succeeded in carrying out relatively little mischief here, though the menace grows apace with every passing year. Can you imagine a more bizarre plot than the bombing of the Greenwich Observatory? How utterly senseless."

"Indeed, it is," I responded vehemently, feeling indignation rise within me.

The Prime Minister's eyes seemed to narrow with great intensity upon the topic at hand.

"The Special Crimes Division has got wind of a plot among certain Hibernian fanatics to compound the potential trouble that is brewing in those frozen wastes of our North American Empire. God knows, my poor nephew has borne the brunt of endless defamation at the hands of those quick to judge but slow to offer feasible alternatives. Bloody Balfour, indeed!"[5]

His voice trailed off, and Holmes and I allowed the silence to hang menacingly in the shadows of the alcove. In a moment or two—although I confess it seemed like fifteen—the marquis continued.

---

[5]   A. J. Balfour was chief secretary for Ireland, 1887–1891. He enforced the Crime Act vigorously, earning the epithet, "Bloody Balfour."

"The word is that a lawless band of Fenians are preparing to embarrass Britannic interests in the Canadian north, disrupt the precarious new accord between ourselves and the Americans, and undermine the traditions of loyalty and filial piety our Canadian sons have shown us so readily in the generation since the BNA Act.

"Quite simply, these blackguards intend to spread rumour, provoke selective violence, and foment every sort of mischief to discredit both British intentions and Canadian capabilities for proper order and civilized government.

"We have specific information about one, Patrick the Piper; his true identity has escaped us so far. Unfortunately, our informants lost track of him yesterday in Liverpool. He undoubtedly plans to take passage and plant the tares of chaos among the seedlings of civilization in the Canadian north. The Special Crimes Division identified him as a cold-blooded and ruthless killer, recently associated with continental anarchists and presumably schooled in the diabolical instruments of heartless, random destruction, calculated to shake the very foundations of society and its institutions. Some men of substance may find the Anarchist Club in Berner Street[6] amusing–what with their cries of "Awake, ye men of toil"–but I can assure you that dynamite is not amusing in the hands of a wild-eyed fanatic."

Holmes and I could do nothing but nod our agreement as the great presence seemed to empty himself of these pressing anxieties. Remarkably, despite the obvious depth of feeling, his voice had not risen above the whispered modulation with which he had begun.

"Sad it is," he continued, "that men such as this Patrick, first stirred by the Irish Republican Brotherhood, or even the likes of Yeats or Synge, should be exposed to the more virulent venom of foreign degenerates to whom the traditional values of British fair play are utterly unknown, and even the object of scorn and derision. We English could arrive at a reasoned and just understanding with our other island if it were not for

---

[6] The Berner Street Club's membership included Whitechapel radicals, many associated with the Rose Street Communist Club. Berner Street was also the site of one of Jack the Ripper's murders in 1888.

the alien ideas and accursed atrocities imported from the lands of the autocrats and tartars.

"Mangled bodies and maimed and mutilated innocents have become the vehicle of protest that the dissidents and malcontents of our day have adopted. The infernal devices that once seemed to be confined to the evil hands of Slavic syndicalists, I fear, may become the instruments that the feverish fanatics among the Gaels may adopt.

"And this man, Patrick the Piper, has mastered all the diabolical skills of these elements to further the misguided ideals he has adopted regarding his troubled land. What is most alarming is that he has eluded our surveillance."

Again the Prime Minister paused, as if to let his words sink in. For my part, I began to understand the gravity of the situation. Holmes seemed very intense, as intense as I had ever seen him. His nimble mind undoubtedly was racing ahead, evaluating the implications of what we were being told.

"Britannic authority undermined, Canadian jurisdiction will be challenged. American tempers will flair. The demand for the protection of American citizens will call for extending the presence of the Stars and Stripes where now the Union Jack flies." Holmes shot out the words like the fusillade of a Maxim gun.

"Exactly," replied the marquis.

"But is not Canadian authority enough to foil whatever devilish schemes this Irish madman may be hatching?" I asked.

"There are, of course, some very capable colonials on the scene," he concurred. "I must tell you frankly, however, Her Majesty's Government would feel inestimably more at ease if your notable skills–those of genuine Englishmen–were turned to the task of foiling this desperate man and his demonic plots." The latter was directed to my colleague, of course.

"Colonials are never quite like real Englishmen," the PM added, shaking his noble head slightly.

"At any rate, one cannot have too many lines of defence against the threat of random violence," Holmes said.

"You are precisely right," His Lordship nodded. "Your reputation for incisiveness is well deserved. Who can guess the horrors to be let loose? American citizens dead and wounded. American property destroyed. Make no mistake. Americans hold their property more dearly than even we do.

"Can you imagine the clamour for protection and justice raised by the Americans? Their outraged cries would resound from the Chilkoot to the Potomac. And how it would be heard in Washington! Since Randolph of Virginia called for the annexation of Canada in the early decades of this century, the most ambitious of the expansionists have cast covetous eyes north of the 49th parallel."

"Even today's papers verify that Yankee expansionist ambitions are global," Holmes interjected. (His allusion was, I believe, to the article in the *Times* that Mrs Hudson had placed dutifully before Holmes's door this morning–"American soldiers applying the 'water cure' to rebellious Filipinos who seemed to fear that the unfurling of the American flag was far from temporary." But then that was the South Seas, not British North America.)

"Precisely," Salisbury nodded, "and we must see to it that the Yukon does not become another Texas, California, or Oregon."

The marquis stood to his feet. His penetrating eyes peered intently at me briefly and then shifted to Holmes. He drew a pocket watch from the ample girth of his waistcoat, snapped the cover open, closed it decisively, and took a step towards my colleague. Holmes seemed about to rise, but the corpulent bulk of the Prime Minister prevented his doing so momentarily.

"Are the Canadian authorities to be advised of our involvement?" Holmes asked, rising somewhat awkwardly from beneath the noble presence.

It is decided then. Holmes is accepting the request. Or had it been a command? England had always expected that every man would do his duty.

The Prime Minister's hushed but earnest voice broke my momentary reverie. "I think we must. The colonials are very sensitive these days.

Proudly British, you know, but keenly determined to establish a Canadian identity. We must be careful not to give offense. But your primary contact will be with our man from Special Crimes Division, who is acquainted with the devilish depths to which this breed of criminal will stoop."

As the marquis stepped back, a shaft of sunlight dramatically highlighted his countenance; this was certainly a man accustomed to leading men.

"Mr Holmes, Her Majesty's Government would be most grateful if you could clear your calendar and extend us your help."

"My Lord, whatever modest skills I may have are at the disposal of Her Majesty and her Government," Holmes responded without a second's delay.

"Thank you," our host responded warmly. "This will, of course, involve travel—some of it of a rather arduous nature, I fear."

The Prime Minister glanced at me, and I must confess, I drew in my stomach rather self-consciously.

"You will wish Dr Watson to accompany you. Arrangements can be made for expense vouchers and appropriate travel documents. Time is of the essence in this matter. I do hope that an early date for your departure will be possible."

"Watson and I shall expedite matters here at home. I am certain my colleague will be able to spare the time. His practice is presently, shall we say, not very demanding. What do you say?" he asked, turning to me.

The honour of such a call to duty, coming as it did directly from the Prime Minister, flattered me considerably, I must admit. The august presence loomed expectantly over us in the alcove. Protocol seemed to call for us to stand, as His Lordship had, but Holmes could scarcely move from his seat for the ample waistcoated girth of Her Majesty's first minister, who regarded us intently and at very close hand. I stood to my feet, mumbling my concurrence without fully grasping the dimensions of the assignment with which we had been presented. As I have noted elsewhere, my experiences in Afghanistan had admirably prepared me for quick departures and readiness for new duties at a moment's notice.

"Naturally, Mr Holmes," I answered, squaring my shoulders with, I trust, some forgivable pride.

As we passed the Reform Club, hard by the Travellers, Holmes mused idly over the remarkable role that such institutions played in the ongoing course of public affairs. "That matters of such weighty consequence should be aired and such vitally significant decisions should be reached within their walls is remarkable," said he.

Reflecting on the ominous import of what we had just heard, I proceeded to remark upon the dire consequences that a large American immigration seemed so often to have. "Annexation has followed such influx with great regularity," I observed.

"Don't forget, however," my colleague injected, "that poor Kruger in South Africa found the presence of growing numbers of uitlanders, most of whom were British, alarming, and only the prelude to the extinguishing of Boer sovereignty."

Poor Kruger, I thought with a mild sense of outrage. Poor Kruger, indeed! This was not a very patriotic observation for Mr Holmes to make, given the current unpleasantness in the veldt. But I suppose he was right, though at this very time, our statesmen were seeking a means out of the present impasse at Bloemfontein.[7]

---

[7] A reference to the meeting of the British High Commissioner, Lord Milner, with the Boer President to settle disputes in the Rand between Boers and English immigrants in May 1899.

SS CANADA

As I set my Gladstone bag on the kerb, a hansom cab deposited Sherlock Holmes a few feet from me. The press of the crowd arriving at the station made it difficult for me to make my presence known, and my eminent friend stood for a moment or two surveying the crush of humanity before I was able to elbow my way to him.

"Ah good, Watson," he smiled. "I see you are here in good time. The Liverpool train does not depart for five and twenty minutes, and as we have our tickets, we will not be pressed to make it."

The two days since our interview with the Prime Minister had been packed with hectic activity. A passport in the name of William Housman issued to Holmes bore Holmes's likeness, while I was now in possession of one in the name of Dr John Wallace. I felt some consternation at the deceit being perpetrated by these documents, and yet I understood fully the need for such a measure on our Government's part. As the Prime Minister had pointed out ruefully, honesty and forthrightness were seriously under attack in this day and age.

Our baggage was modest considering the journey on which we were about to embark. Though the assistance of porters made it no problem at Paddington Station, the likelihood was that, before this venture was over, Holmes and I would be required to wrestle our own bulky portmanteaus and duffel bags. So we sought to keep the impedimenta to a minimum. Nonetheless, it represented a fair mound before the iron gates of the terminal.

With the assistance of an eager young man who approached us with a handcart and a ceremonious doffing of his cap, our luggage was soon transferred to the noisy vastness of the station. Despite the relative brightness of the day, the interior was cloaked in a grey luminescence. But my spirit soared as we approached the platform by which the Liverpool Express stood. I could not help but recall the excitement that had gripped me those long years ago as I'd embarked for India. This was surely to be an adventure to rival that.

Compared to the crowded accommodations on that voyage of long ago, this one promised to be the essence of comfort, indeed luxury. Our passage was booked on the new pride of the White Star Lines, the *Oceanic*. My reverie was ended abruptly by the wheezing discharge of steam from the locomotive far down the platform, followed by a shuddering response from the coaches. Holmes and I climbed aboard with dispatch. With a further complaining groan, our train moved off and out from under the iron and glass canopy. Heavy rain from a passing shower now beat upon the windows of out compartment. Holmes drew his pipe from his pocket and settled into the seat with evident satisfaction. Our long journey had begun.

Until our transatlantic voyage was complete, there was little we could do, and our instructions left us pretty much to ourselves until such time as we reached Montreal. There, a contact, privy to our mission would render us assistance and perhaps accompany us. It was our understanding, however, that we were embarking upon a task of which few in official circles were aware and that would remain hidden forever from the general public.

As our train rushed northward, Holmes busied himself with an assortment of documents, memoranda, and maps that he devoured with singular intensity. Only occasionally did he raise his head to mutter a terse observation or instruction to me.

"Our Montreal contact will make himself known by enquiring whether we are the two gentlemen who require transportation to Gatineau. To this we are to reply, 'Thank you, no. But we are going to Ottawa. Is it nearby?' Our man will then respond, 'Ottawa is just across the river.'"

"How will he identify us?" I asked.

"You are to carry a copy of Steevens's *With Kitchener to Khartoum* in your right hand and I ... I, Watson, shall carry this magnificent new otter skin hat, with which I intend to protect my ears from the chilling winds of the Canadian north." With that, Holmes produced as fine a fur hat as can be imagined, complete with earflaps that promised shelter from the coldest arctic blast. With a puckish chuckle, he placed it atop his head for a brief moment. The sight of Holmes in this frontier headpiece, as our railway carriage traversed the green and eminently civilized landscape of Oxfordshire, was truly incongruous but not without its delights.

"And why *With Kitchener to Khartoum*?" I asked.

"Admittedly an arbitrary choice. But widely read here and in the Dominions—wherever the pride of empire prevails. Nothing to attract particular attention, but a ready means of identification."

"And may our humble contributions to Her Britannic Majesty's affairs be in small measure as successful as those of the great Sirdar," I reflected fervently. "Omdurman was a proud moment!"

"But will it always be seen as such? I wonder." Holmes closed his eyes and leaned back with a slight sigh.

The Liverpool wharves were awash with every conceivable specimen of humankind. Steerage passengers with their shapeless bundles of personal effects struggled into the steamship terminals with resigned determination, small children in wide-eyed wonder bearing their share. Hansoms deposited the more affluent, while the occasional shining landau or other fine coach, complete with footmen, provided a more spectacular arrival for the well-to-do.

Holmes and I found our way to the White Star facilities, where we intended to board the *Oceanic*, newly commissioned and the second of her name to fly the White Star flag. To our disappointment, however, a confusion in bookings left us without passage. Holmes took the matter with apparent calm, but I sensed his agitation concerning the prospect of delay in getting to our urgent task. How such an error could have occurred was beyond me, but we now had to make other arrangements with all haste.

Leaving our baggage in the care of the baggage agent, Holmes set off with his familiar long stride to resolve our quandary. I should have thought that a request to Her Majesty's Government would have quickly provided space aboard the magnificent vessel now berthed at the White Star pier. But within the hour, my companion miraculously had booked us on the Dominion Line Steamship, the *Canada*. She was the largest and most luxurious of the line's fleet, though her nine thousand-ton displacement was modest in comparison to the *Oceanic*. Viewing her graceful lines pleasantly surprised us, and upon boarding her, we found her accommodations very adequate. We were, indeed, fortunate that this ship was in port and bound for Montreal on tomorrow's tide.

As the *Canada* sailed southwest to round Kinsale Head, Holmes studied the horizon and the approaching headlands of the Irish coast, nudging through the dissolving fog. The boat deck was empty except for the two of us, it being breakfast time aboard ship.

"The steward just issued last call," I reiterated to my preoccupied friend.

"Yes, yes," Holmes responded, turning from the distant vista to transfix me with his penetrating gaze. "It occurs to me that our mishandled bookings may have been no accident."

"Really, Holmes? Is it possible that our peregrinations are already known to the enemy?"

"If I had any reason whatsoever to suspect the evil hand of Moriarty in this—"

"Moriarty!" I exclaimed.

"I know, it's preposterous. It is simply that the most innocent coincidence may sometimes be the product of diabolical scheming." Holmes's lean fingers intertwined as he pressed his hands against his chin in thought. "But we are on our way at any rate, and we should avail ourselves of an excellent Dominion Lines breakfast."

As we left the railing, a course adjustment brought a cold rush of wind and wisps of fog along the deck which, together with thoughts of Moriarty, caused me to draw my collar more closely around my neck.

The *Canada* made a steady fifteen knots, and the relatively calm seas made for pleasant sailing. The North Atlantic was remarkably calm for a springtime voyage, and I experienced only the slightest discomfort from the gentle rolling of the ship. Our cabin was more than adequate, especially in comparison to the accommodations that I had enduring during that trip to India so many years ago. Holmes continued to spend a great deal of time engrossed in reading the considerable bundle of papers he drew from the bottom of his Gladstone bag.

"Here," he said, looking up from the small desk by the porthole. "You might familiarize yourself with some of the forces at play in our little assignment—a report from the select committee on Fenian violence to begin with then this material on the Alaskan boundary issue, and some Canada First literature."

A current issue of the *Canadian Magazine* caught my attention. The editor was clearly distressed by the present direction of immigration policy. "Is Canada to become as rude, as uncultured, as fickle, as heterogeneous, as careless of law and order and good citizenship as the United States?" he demanded.

Delving into the materials Holmes had passed to me, I began to grasp something of the complexities at play in the case before us. I was aroused abruptly from my thoughts, however, by my companion's sharp and insistent voice.

"Dr Wallace, Dr John Wallace," he cried.

"What the deuce, Holmes!" I answered in alarm.

"No, no, no," he continued as loudly as before.

"I'm sorry, old man. I can't for the life of me—"

"Dr Wallace—that is your name on your passport, and that is your name for the duration of this assignment. You must not forget it for a moment. It must become second nature to you. You must respond reflexively to it. One slip, and our entire artifice is gone."

"Of course, Holmes, of course."

"No, no, no, Dr Wallace. It is Mr Housman. Nothing else must pass between us, even when we are entirely alone. It must be second nature."

"Yes. Mr William Housman," I responded deliberately and with determination, seeking to print the lesson indelibly on my mind. The habits of many years of association are not easy to break in a matter of days.

Having made his point forcefully, Holmes (or should I say Housman?) settled back to relight his pipe. I renewed my survey of the materials that now sat in an uneven stack on the cabin floor, more aware than ever of the gravity of our task. But the empire was indeed fortunate to have the services of so thorough and incisive a mind as that of Mr Sherlock Holmes.

Nothing but the occasional rustle of paper broke the silence of our stateroom for the next several hours. Only as the late afternoon light began to fade and a perceptible increase in the roll and pitch of our quarters made us aware of the rising sea, did either of us stir from our preoccupation.

On our fifth day at sea, Mr Housman and Dr Wallace were invited to take their evening meal at the captain's table. The ship's dining room was modest in size but well appointed. Service was excellent and the food very passable. Two days of heavy seas had left me too queasy to eat much, and the same seemed to be true of Holmes, whose alias was now firmly imprinted in my mind, and, I trust, my conversation.

"Captain Hawke at your service, gentlemen," announced the tall mariner, immaculate in white dress uniform, arriving at the table just as we did.

Already seated were an elderly couple by the name of Paget, a clergyman and his wife. Beside them sat a retired guardsman on holidays to visit a brother in Ontario and a Lloyd's underwriter. Introductions completed, Captain Hawke demonstrated the social graces required of the master of a passenger liner in this modern age of travel. Conversation flowed easily.

"This may well be one of the last passages this ship will make across the North Atlantic for some time," he confided with candour. "Her owners have been advised that the Government may seek to press her into service as a troop ship in the unhappy event that we find ourselves at war with the South African Boers."

"Will Canada join in such a war?" asked the guardsman. "She will, though not all are happy about the prospect," answered Hawke.

"An understatement, I suspect," said Holmes. "The Quebec Frenchmen will not see this as their affair."

"What shall become of our Empire?" asked the clergyman. "Such an unhappy encounter with the Boer will surely destroy the nobility of our cause."

"Britain will no longer be great if she backs down before a band of Kaffir-beaters," the ex-guardsman injected.

"Are our ideals to be sacrificed at the altar of material interest and martial power?" asked the clergyman somewhat heatedly.

Captain Hawke, seeking to avoid unpleasantness among his table guests, ardently commended the main course that our waiter now placed before us. The coq au vin was excellent, and my appetite had returned.

The cleric, however, seemed eager to talk about more than the culinary output of the galley. "The Americans who denounce our empire seem to have developed a new and alarming taste for empire of their own," he asserted, wiping his chin meticulously with the linen serviette.

"Indeed they have," the captain concurred. "Their little war with Spain promises rich territorial rewards for the Yankees. And once the appetite is whetted, it will likely turn, as it has so often before, to British North America. The expansionists are loose again I fear."

"Preserve the empire, I say," said the guardsman, "South Africa or North America. God save the Queen."

"The Queen," I intoned, raising my glass to the table guests.

"The Queen," they murmured, joining in the toast.

After a brief pause, the Lloyd's underwriter, who to this point had said nothing, spoke. "But Canadians and Americans are essentially the same. I can't tell them apart, frankly."

"Never let it be said," quipped Captain Hawke. "Actually, Canadians have a hard time making up their minds about the States. Some, like Goldwin Smith, expect and welcome union with their southern neighbours. But most Canadians have no desire to be absorbed by the American leviathan. I think Sir Oliver Mowat was right when he said that Canada has but two choices—annexation to the United States or strong connection with Britain. Personally, I'm for the latter."

So, despite Captain Hawke's efforts to turn the evening's conversation to lighter topics, his dinner guests made politics the focus of their attention. Holmes desisted from any comment, and I took his lead and refrained from making any observations, although our recent reading had been most germane to the issues at hand. It seemed to me the empire was at a crossroads.

"The clergyman," said Holmes, as we returned to our cabin, "I find less than convincing. Having once assumed such a guise myself, I find his benevolent air contrived."

I chuckled at my recollection of Holmes's brilliant impersonation of a simple-minded cleric those years ago in the case of Irene Adler and the king of Bohemia.[8]

"You don't suppose—"

"We cannot be too cautious," said Holmes, entering our dimly lit quarters with a brief backwards glance along the empty corridor.

As the good ship *Canada* entered the Gulf of St. Lawrence, I leaned expectantly upon the forward rail of the boat deck, straining for my first glance of Britain's oldest Dominion. It was a moment or two before I realized that Holmes had joined me silently. For a long time we stood studying the western horizon. Our ten days of relative idleness at sea would come to an end within a few hours. We had occupied a good deal of time in acquainting ourselves more fully with the players in this game

---

8   "A Scandal in Bohemia," *The Strand Magazine*, July 1891.

of international intrigue, but I could sense in my colleague a restlessness that now craved action.

Faintly in the distance, a pale purple line crept upward beyond the grey-green waters. Terra firma was always a welcome sight to the oceanic voyager. My spirits lifted.

"Canada," said Holmes quietly. "Canada. I believe the name is derived from an Indian word for a collection of huts. Let us hope that there is something more substantial holding these provinces together."

"Good heavens, Holmes. I should think this young nation has the very brightest future. Was it not their Prime Minister, Laurier, who just said that the twentieth century will belong to Canada," I expostulated.

"Quite right. I can see that you have been assiduous in digesting the material I brought along–and a good deal more. And again, I remind you, the name is Housman. Even in moments of agitation–especially then–we must not forget our *noms de guerre*."

I apologized once more, feeling somewhat depressed by my error, although it was the first time in three days that I had allowed the name of the world's leading consulting detective to pass my lips. We had, all this time, enjoyed the solitude of the forward boat deck, but several passengers now were ascending the steps to our level.

Very perceptibly now, the jaws of the mighty St. Lawrence began to constrict as we sailed westward in near perfect weather and ideal maritime conditions, particularly considering the reputation of this region at the vernal equinox. As salubrious as the season seemed, sizable fingers of snow still reached down here and there to grasp at the passing waters.

"Will our contact be aware of our changed travel arrangements?" I asked.

"A coded message to Whitehall took care of that before our embarkation. But the key question is, who else knows?"

As we proceeded up the St. Lawrence, the pattern of fence lines and narrow fields, running at right angles to the river and disappearing beyond the gentle rise on our starboard, provided mute reminder of the *habitant* origins of agriculture in this region.

"So green," I exclaimed, "and yet so unlike the English countryside."

"Yes, but Gallic traditions are struggling to survive in more than just the pattern of farming practices. We can only hope that the malcontents who are behind the present business do not tap the latent discontent that festers in this province."

Our sea voyage was almost over. The great cliffs of Quebec slipped by as we made our way to the dining room for our last evening meal aboard ship. I thought of Wolfe and Montcalm and, with satisfaction, saw the Union Jack atop the citadel. The sturdy walls, bathed in the golden hues of the setting sun, seemed to represent stability and security.

"Sir Henry Baskerville always spoke most fondly of his years in Canada," Holmes reflected.

We were seated alone, the majority of the passengers having apparently foregone this sitting.

"Yes. I often thought he regretted having to return to England," I ventured.

The mention of Sir Henry reminded me of the manuscript that I hoped to soon begin, relating the details of that most remarkable case. The rough notes I had scribbled at Dartmoor even now lay locked in my desk drawer. I would have to return to them soon, as my publisher had already expressed impatience for the first instalment. I think I will call it *The Hound of the Baskervilles.*[9]

"I hope our absence does not occasion too much curiosity," I remarked, as my mind strayed back to Baker Street and our more accustomed line of duties and routine.

"Mrs Hudson understands we are enjoying a well-earned rest in Cornwall."

The steamship Canada berthed at the Quai Victoria in the early morning hours. The haste and confusion of debarkation was compounded by the semi-darkness, as well as the unpleasantness of a

---

[9] Henry was the nephew of Sir Charles and his heir. *The Hound of the Baskervilles*, London, 1902. Watson completed the story upon his return, and it appeared in serialized form in *The Strand Magazine* from August 1901 to April 1902.

chilling rain with intermittent waves of sleet. The excellent weather we had enjoyed during the entire crossing had come abruptly to an end here in Montreal.

The uniformed customs and immigration officers looked almost familiar. Clearly, we were under the aegis of Her Britannic Majesty, whose noble visage was displayed prominently on the back wall of the cavernous customs shed, draped with red, white, and blue bunting. My spirit swelled with pride.

"The empire is a splendid expression of Anglo-Saxon civilization—our gift to the world," I said.

Customs and immigration mercifully proved routine. Presenting false documents and entering the daughter dominion in such a clandestine manner did not settle well with my conscience. Holmes, I gathered, accepted it as an unfortunate necessity. At any rate, as we gathered our baggage, Holmes withdrew the otter-skin cap from his valise and planted it firmly on his head.

"Your copy of *With Kitchener at Khartoum*," said Holmes.

"Oh yes, of course," I mumbled, placing the book conspicuously in my right hand.

The crowd of arriving passengers surged around us like a human tide, making the prospect of our being spotted by our contact seem remote. A porter addressed us in French, seeking to assist us to a carriage.

"Merci. Mais non," Holmes answered, surveying the chaotic array of faces that engulfed us, intent on finding a cab, spotting family or friends, or simply trying to take the measure of this new land that they now would learn to call their home. The din of tongues and dialects struck me as a veritable Babel. Even the varieties of our mother tongue beat strangely on my ears.

"Carry your luggage, sir," a red-capped boy shouted.

"No. No thank you," said Holmes, with a slight look of annoyance towards the lad.

"I see little prospect that our man will find us very quickly in this press," I observed.

"Perhaps. Unfortunately, a cap such as mine is not so rare a piece of apparel here," Holmes said with a faint smile.

"Are you two gentlemen needing transportation to Gatineau?"

We turned to see a ruddy-faced red-headed man of average height who stood enquiringly at my shoulder.

"Thank you, no. But we are going to Ottawa. Is it nearby?" Holmes responded.

"Ah, so 'tis you, sirs," the stranger said. His accent and appearance were as Irish as one would ever encounter. "The name is Cromwell Devlin, Special Crimes Division, at your service. And you are ... eh, Mr Housman and Dr Wallace?"

"Correct. And you have a very sharp eye to spot us so quickly in this press," said Holmes.

Handshakes and pleasantries were hurried in the jostling crowd.

"Let me assist you, gentlemen. I have a cart waiting in the street, if the rascal has not accepted another fare."

MONTREAL

The wind and sleet chilled us as we reached the curb, where a rather primitive wagonette stood. Devlin helped us load our impedimenta while the shaggy dapple-grey pawed restlessly at the cobblestones. As Holmes and I climbed aboard the conveyance, the dour driver snapped the reins and, with a loud but indecipherable command, we lurched forward. Devlin clung precariously for a moment before successfully gaining the seat beside the driver. Fresh gusts of sleet buffeted us on a wind that seemed to have arrived directly from the polar cap.

"The 200 block on St. Paul's Street East," Devlin ordered.

"I should prefer a hansom," Holmes muttered under his breath.

"There's some who might call this a democrat," responded the driver, apparently overhearing the remark.

"It's not far. We're booked at Rasco's Hotel. And a fine hotel it is. At one time, said to be the finest on the continent, with a register groaning with the names of the great. Today it's clean and reasonable and handy to the train station," Devlin offered cheerfully.

"A democrat," said I lightly, reflecting on the driver's comment. "The Yanks would like to see more of these about, no doubt. But it is gratifying to know Her Britannic Majesty still reigns over this land."

"Yes, Dr Wallace," Holmes replied with a deliberateness that seemed to call for an end to that line of conversation.

"Not all the Frenchies would share your enthusiasm," Devlin called over his shoulder.

"Nor some others," Holmes stated with finality.

Our progress was slow amid the jumble of conveyances that disgorged from the harbour, and we had not gone far when Holmes suddenly commanded the driver to stop.

"Here, is this not the famous Bonsecour Church?" he asked.

"Yes," the man replied with an edge in his voice.

"Good. Let us stop for a moment and have a look," Holmes ordered.

This seemed a strange command indeed. I had never known my colleague to have a particular interest in ecclesiastical architecture, and at this early hour and under these less than pleasant conditions, the whim seemed perverse.

With some grumbling, the driver drew the dapple out of traffic and to the kerb.

"Come, Dr Wallace, Mr Devlin, let us take a few moments to inspect this splendid old church. I believe it is frequently and fondly referred to as 'the sailor's chapel.' It's the oldest church in Montreal, if I am not mistaken."

The three of us entered the Roman arched door and stood for a time as our eyes adjusted to the dim interior. It was, indeed, a lovely old structure, but I was utterly at a loss to understand Holmes's sudden fascination with this particular sanctuary. I stepped several feet down the aisle, Devlin somewhat behind me, while Holmes lingered momentarily in the narthex. I would have proceeded further had not Holmes recalled us. As my vision finally penetrated the shadowy recesses, I could just observe some ship models, apparently contributed by grateful sailors.

"Many a sailor has found solace in this place," Holmes quietly reflected, "but we shouldn't keep our driver waiting. He does not strike me as a very obliging fellow."

For the life of me, Holmes's stop at Bonsecours Church was a most inexplicable event, but we were soon deposited at Rasco's, and I dismissed it from mind. Devlin, with great efficiency, managed our baggage; Holmes paid the driver; and we entered the lobby.

The desk clerk, in a most accommodating manner, assured us that our rooms were ready and available immediately. With a flourish he produced room keys from the pigeonholes behind the desk.

"A wash up, a bit of breakfast, and a rest will put you gentlemen in first-class order, I reckon. Get your land legs back, and I'll be at your service. Dalhousie Station is nearby, and we can catch the transcontinental train tomorrow if you like."

I awoke in mid afternoon, pleasantly surprised to see the sun streaming through the window. Holmes was sitting at the small desk against the far wall of our room.

Noting that I had awakened, he turned and said, "Refreshed, are you not? I shall be back shortly. I wish to send a coded cable to London. If Devlin comes by, tell him I've gone for a walk."

With that, he gathered the paper from the blotter before him and was gone. I bestirred myself from the comfort of the bed, remarkably refreshed. A shave would certainly be in order, so I rummaged through my duffel for razor and shaving mug. My face was fully lathered when a knock came at the door.

"Come in," I called.

"Well, doctor, Canada is putting on a better face for ye now," Devlin commented cheerfully as he stepped into the room. "And what would ye be fancying for supper? Hello… where's the man?" Devlin looked towards Holmes's bed, rumpled but clearly empty.

"Off for a walk," said I.

"Well now, an energetic fellow, this colleague of yours. No matter. I've checked the schedules. We can be heading west tomorrow if you gents feel up to it."

"I should think that will be fine. The sooner to the task the better. If these enemies of civilization, decency, and order are to be stopped, we have no time to pamper ourselves. I for one am ready to proceed."

The vehemence with which I made this assertion caused me to cut my chin.

"Will you be kind enough to hand me the bag there by my duffel. I need a bit of mild astringent," I said, wiping the remaining lather from my neck.

"Well, doctor," Devlin chuckled, "I trust you're more deft with a scalpel than a cutthroat–or, as they say here, a straight razor."

The remark seemed barbed, but I let it go. Devlin had a disarming smile as he settled himself by the window. I am never quite able to fathom a Celt.

It was five and twenty past five when Holmes returned. I was now becoming accustomed to the otter cap, and somehow, it seemed quite appropriate to our surrounding and mission. Still, there was no mistaking the essential Englishness of my colleague. I hoped we would not be too conspicuous in this land. Fortunately, the large numbers of our countrymen who arrived daily prevented our presence from occasioning any particular attention. This was, after all, a part of the British Empire.

"Perhaps now that Dr Wallace and I are rested and somewhat refreshed, you can briefly explain your assignment," Holmes suggested. "My colleague and I are most anxious to be at the business at hand."

"My job is to see you to your destination and look to your needs. Orders from on high are that I–I think the top man said expedite–that I expedite your journey, Mr Housman."

"Your assistance will be gratefully accepted, though Wallace and I are accustomed to attending to our own needs," Holmes responded.

"Contrary to what many believe about English gentlemen, neither of us employs a manservant–except, of course, for my batsman in India," I added.

"My duty is but to serve Her Majesty," Devlin stated modestly.

"Mr Devlin has checked the train schedules, and we can leave tomorrow," I said, anxious that he not feel slighted.

"Well, sir, you are indeed efficient in looking to arrangements. It looks as if London has chosen well."

"Thank you, sir. Cromwell Devlin can find no greater satisfaction than in seeing the cause advanced in any way his humble self can find to do." Devlin bowed low and smiled.

"Fine sentiments, indeed. But if I may ask, what brought you to Special Crimes, Mr Devlin?" asked Holmes.

"'Tis a bit of a story, and I'll not bother you with the details. Irish I may be, but British to the core. My family served King Billie, as I do Vicki today. 'Twas '90 when my great-great-granddaddy fell mortally wounded before the banners of Orange that fateful day. Aye, the Boyne ran red with his blood, but he and the other brave lads saved our land from darkness and falsehood. Nor was he the last of my kin to pay the price. Not ten years past, my poor uncle Ned dead. Struck with a paving stone as he marched behind the Lambeg drums."

"Your home was where, Mr Devlin?" asked Holmes. "I'll warrant you hail from County Antrim."

"Close. But no. From Derry. From the fair town of Derry, sir. And proud of it!"

"Ah, yes. That would be right," Holmes rejoined with a smile.

The brief recitation seemed to confirm that Mr Cromwell Devlin was indeed a man with a cause. The troubles that had so long plagued England's other island seemed to have left a spirit of crusading zeal in the man that shone through his keen blue eyes. He sat now on the sill of the window of our hotel room and gazed intently into the street below. I suspect he was not seeing the grey cobblestones of St. Paul's Street but some familiar scene, glorious and tragic, from his natal land.

Disrupting Devlin's reverie, Holmes asked, "I presume you are aware of the primary object of our concern—the one known as Patrick the Piper."

"And a scoundrel he is," said Devlin.

"Descriptions are meagre, but his record for violence is not," Holmes rejoined.

"Special Crimes gets only rumours. An elusive fellow, our Mr Patrick," Devlin said.

"And he is said to have slipped through everyone's hands and is now somewhere in this country," said Holmes.

"We have many informants, but just how trustworthy they may be is another question," Devlin observed. "They say he's been seen in Montreal, Hull, Ottawa, and Three Rivers, but who knows? And we must remember, it's not easy to conduct business here without giving offense to the locals."

"We are well aware of the delicacy of our position, and we shall do all we can to respect and satisfy the aspirations of the senior daughter Dominion," said Holmes. "Compounding our problem is the fact that enemies of the Crown are not lacking here … especially here!" he added ominously.

We both turned and looked at him expectantly. But apparently that was all that Holmes intended to say, for he proceeded to rummage through his pockets, withdrawing his tobacco pouch and scanning the oaken dresser for his pipe, which lay amid a considerable clutter of toiletries and miscellaneous personal effects.

"If you were an Irish republican, where would you seek assistance in this city?" he finally asked, as a thick cloud of smoke circled his head.

"Undoubtedly, there are lots of rascals long established here," I said with a rising sense of indignation.

"And I believe the Sulpicians have had a long and friendly relationship with the Irish," Holmes added. "Indeed, old St. Patrick's once stood not far from here, if I am not mistaken. The Sulpicians served the Micks well."

I was amazed again at the store of Holmes's information, though after all these years, it should not have seemed at all surprising.

"Of course, one could recite almost endlessly the possible allies that a foe of the Crown might find here. The point is, we cannot possibly ferret out the evasive Patrick the Piper in this city. But we do know his destination, and we can anticipate his route with some degree of confidence. At some point, our paths should intersect if our reasoning is sound enough."

"Good heavens, Hol—, good heavens, Housman," I cried. "This is such a vast continent, almost beyond imagining, I confess. We have only a name, with almost no description. We know he intends evil, but the nature of the evil is unknown to us. How and where shall we choke off this diabolical plot?"

"The first step you have taken already, my friend. You have recognized the enormity of the task."

"Aye," affirmed Devlin, "it is a big task."

Deep shadows dominated the street below. The late spring storm was spent. The incandescent light, apparently recently installed in our room, to judge by the fresh patchwork in the plaster, cast brooding shadows across the countenances of my companions.

"For the moment, our immediate task is to discover a suitable eating place," said Holmes, rising to stretch his lengthy frame.

Darkness had fallen by the time we had eaten our evening meal, taken at a rather ordinary establishment called the Chez O'Malley—an unlikely concatenation of Gallic and Gaelic, perhaps symbolizing the task at hand. As we returned to our hotel, I happened to glimpse a most unusual sight. Through the basement window of a noisy and obviously popular canteen, one could see a group of men clad in dungarees and flannel shirts dancing to the wheezing of an accordion. But what was remarkable was the fact that two large brown bears with floral garlands about their necks were whirling about in the dancers' midst, in close approximation to the rhythm of the polka being rendered by a shaggy haired musician.

"Amazing," I muttered, pausing to watch the spectacle.

"Aye, but the proprietor keeps a buffalo that can count to ten," Devlin chuckled. "Of course, he does it with his hoof, but he's a smart animal anyway."

"Canada is still a very young land. Her frontier spirit is obvious. Even here, in Montreal, one can sense that we stand on the remote edge of civilization, poised at the gates of the wilderness," I observed.

"Well said," injected Holmes, "but an evening in Soho produces just as remarkable revelry, as you well know."

We continued down the street, but as we reached the hotel entrance, Holmes suddenly paused, glancing at his pocket watch.

"You and Devlin will want to turn in. I feel the need for a little more fresh air. I shall be back directly."

With that, he was gone, fur hat resolutely secured as he disappeared beyond the arc of the street lamp.

"Your colleague seems a man of impulse," said Devlin, looking thoughtfully down the now-vacant street.

"I have long since stopped questioning his actions," I answered. "Years of experience have shown me that few things he does without good reason."

The warmth of the hotel lobby made me realize how chilly it had become outside. Devlin left me in the hall, and I entered our room, grateful for the chance to remove my boots and place my weary feet upon the once elegant ottoman, a reminder of the Rasco's past glories.

I must have drifted off for a few moments, for I was awakened by the sound of Holmes's key in the latch. Dropping his cape and otter hat at the foot of the bed, he rubbed his hands vigorously together and blew on them for a moment or two. Then, reaching into an inner pocket, he produced a paper, which appeared to be a telegram.

"I have been in communication with London," he said in a matter-of-fact manner, "and I have some interesting information. Our passage on the SS *Canada* brought us to port some thirty hours after the arrival of the *Oceana*. Our delay was no accident! Moriarty must surely have had a hand in it. His minions are everywhere. It was a small problem to have our bookings mishandled."

"But why? We are here. What has he gained?" I asked. "Intelligence believes that Patrick the Piper arrived aboard the *Oceana*."

"Then he is gone—a jump ahead of us."

"Perhaps," Holmes nodded, "but the evil genius sought more than a few hours advantage for his protégé. He is taunting me, my friend. He is giving me what naughty school boys call 'the Fig.'"

"How so?" I asked.

"The clergyman, Paget, with whom we ate at Captain Hawke's table—he was no man of the cloth. An enquiry to the archbishop's office indicates that no one by that name in holy orders could be sailing to Canada. Last year, the real Reverend Paget was laid to rest in the churchyard at Fenny Stratford—the parish he had served for sixty years."

"Then who and what did—"

"Simply a distraction, designed to test my powers of observation and to lay down a false scent."

"Really, Holmes?" I slipped here, but Holmes ignored it.

"Nor is this likely to be the last," he added grimly. "One soon begins to suspect everyone."

"Not a bad practice. But I have further news. The Prime Minister, aware that our presence in Canada could well become common knowledge, feels we must pay a courtesy call on our Canadian hosts. Both Whitehall and Ottawa are naturally anxious to avoid embarrassment."

"Of course, very understandable," I nodded.

"The Colonial Secretary is particularly uneasy about relationships these days. He and the Prime Minister agree that the appearance of openness and mutual cooperation must be maintained at all costs. You know, of course, Joe's dedication to the ideal of imperial federation. He wants nothing to endanger the atmosphere of good will."

"We surely concur in that," said I. "But this courtesy call–upon whom are we calling?"

"The Prime Minister himself, Sir Wilfred!" Holmes said with a broad grin.

"Well, by Jove, that should prove interesting," I replied with enthusiasm.

"It will be a discreet and private occasion. Neither Devlin nor any other members of the Special Crimes Division who happen to be in this country will participate."

"Why in heaven's name not?" I asked.

"For the very good reason, my friend, that the Canadians are not aware of their presence. That is the way it will continue to be with our discretion and any amount of luck."

"You mean we are to offer our services in the effort to thwart Patrick and his henchmen to reassure our hosts of our forthrightness and good will, while at the same time concealing such important information?" I cried in horror.

"That is exactly it, I'm afraid. Some here will take umbrage enough at the fact that the British Government thinks our assistance necessary, without giving them the impression that Her Majesty's ministers have placed an extensive network of agents from Halifax to Victoria. The senior Dominion prides itself in its competence to deal with all matters of state, both foreign and domestic. It would never do to lead them to think that London thought otherwise."

"But surely, Holmes, you and I cannot—"

"We will, and we must," Holmes interrupted. "And the name is Housman. Do try to avoid those slips. Of course, Laurier and his confidants are aware of our true identity. And, I must say with all due modesty, that the Prime Minister seems eager to meet us. He has let Downing Street know that he has the greatest respect for my reputation. It may appear unduly boastful, but Salisbury's intimations are that few, if any, other personages would have been acceptable for this undertaking."

I took in this assertion with, I trust, excusable pride. What was Johnson without his Boswell? It was, of course, not surprising that the reputation of the world's most famous consulting detective should be as firmly established here as it was on the other side of the Atlantic. The nobility of our assignment made me quite forget the minor deceptions that we would be guilty of with respect to Special Crimes in this land.

"It will be a great honour to meet Sir Wilfred and whomever he makes privy to our mission," I said warmly.

"And we had best see to the condition of our frock coats because we will meet them tomorrow night," Holmes informed me with a twinkle in his eye. "It's off to Ottawa in the morning."

So saying, Holmes proceeded to arrange his bags, sweeping up his cape and hat from the bed to hang them in the small closet by the door. Soon, he was whistling happily in the lavatory, apparently anticipating the morrow's meeting with relish.

That evening, Devlin seemed somewhat chagrined when Holmes informed him of our meeting with the Canadian Prime Minister. The fact that Holmes had contacted London directly caused him to frown deeply as we sat across from each other in a small eating establishment around the corner from Rasco's.

"Well, so it will be yourselves alone who will be meeting with the man, will it?" he asked. "And I suppose Cromwell Devlin is to fade into the background, ready to give you a hand when called for."

"My good fellow, your contributions to Her Majesty's cause will not go un-noted if I have any say in the matter," said I.

"You will understand of course the necessity for discretion on the part of the Colonial Office," said Holmes in a placatory tone.

Devlin took a last swallow of his coffee and smiled his best Gaelic smile. "No offense intended. It's only that my old mother would be proud to think her boy had grasped the hand of so great a man—a Prime Minister, mind you."

"It would not do for the Canadians to get the idea that the mother country did not have full confidence in their ability to run their own affairs. Dr Wallace and I, or should I simply say Watson and I—our true identities are known to Laurier—shall simply present ourselves as two goodwill ambassadors who wish to offer our services in whatever fashion Sir Wilfred should find useful. Salisbury has simply made a fraternal gesture of imperial solidarity."

"Aye. So you'll be catching the train this forenoon. We'd best get you packed and over to Dalhousie Station before long. It would never do to keep your host of the evening waiting."

"I am sorry you cannot meet with the Prime Minister," I said. "Your mother no doubt would have been pleased as you say."

"Aye, well at least she knows I'm doing my duty," Devlin replied. "It will be in Vancouver that I'll see you again, then. Bookings are in order, and lucky we are. Since the spring of '97 it's taken some doing at times to find a seat, not to mention a berth on a sleeping car."

Our baggage assembled, we prepared to head for the station.

OTTAWA

Our train arrived at the Ottawa station in the early evening, after a pleasant trip across the verdant countryside, as lush and tranquil as the Berkshires this time of year. And yet the sheer size of the country was truly remarkable when one considers that the 125 odd miles between Montreal and the capital is a mere trifle in comparison to the entire transcontinental route of the railway. How well I remembered the vastness of North America on my tedious journey to San Francisco some years back.[10]

A very efficient and polite man of middle years greeted us as we stepped from the railway carriage, introducing himself as private secretary to the Prime Minister and expressing his superior's regrets that he had been unable to meet us personally at the station.

"Mr Housman and Dr Wallace, Sir Wilfred asks that you join him for dinner with Mrs Laurier and a few guests. Our brougham is waiting at the curb. The porter will fetch your bags and deliver them," he announced with authority.

The ride from the station, across the Rideau River, and to the Prime Minister's residence on what was known as Sandy Hill was accomplished before darkness had fallen. In the fading light, Laurier's mansion was imposing enough in size but rather ugly in appearance, if I may speak frankly. My initial impressions of the capital were that, while there was an undeniable natural beauty to the city, it had not yet achieved an entirely civilized atmosphere. To the northwest, the

---

[10] See William S. Baring-Gould, *Sherlock Holmes of Baker Street* (New York: Bramhill House, 1962), 299. From January 1884 to August 1886, Watson practiced medicine in San Francisco.

parliament buildings stood in dark silhouette against the fading light of day.

"And what is that pleasant stream?" I enquired of the secretary.

"The Rideau Canal, and beyond, the Ottawa River," he replied.

The silvery sheen of those waters framed a scene of natural magnificence. Holmes and I surveyed it with appreciation. Then we were ushered to the sizable front entrance of the Laurier residence.

"Good evening, gentlemen. It is a pleasure to welcome you to Ottawa, and to the Dominion of the North. My apologies for not meeting you at the station personally, but pressing business and the need for secrecy prevented my doing so."

The immediate impression of the Prime Minister was that of a genuine aristocrat. Wilderness or not, sordid frontier politics or not, Wilfred Laurier had the bearing of a man of quality. His English was magisterial, with a faint hint of French tingeing his pronunciation in a most charming way. He faced Holmes and me in a penetrating but friendly manner. One could readily note a deep intelligence in his eyes. Balding but with an ample shock of grey and white hair above the ears, he could, with justice, be described as handsome. He wore an unusually high collar and a large maroon silk cravat, adorned with a rich pearl stickpin. At a glance, I could understand something of the stir this self-styled "democrat" had created in London social circles in the Diamond Jubilee Year, when he had received a knighthood from Her Gracious Majesty. Small wonder some of their lordships reputedly had been taken aback by the grace and style of this politician from the colonies who showed no hint of the bumpkin about him.

"You are most kind," said Holmes, bowing decorously. Doing likewise, I expressed my deep appreciation. "Your fame has, of course, preceded you to this side of the Atlantic, and we are grateful that your services are now generously to be made available to us. Rest assured that we—that is myself and those within the cabinet privy to your visit—wish to render every assistance to you and Dr Watson while you are in the Dominion. The delicacy of the present situation had led us to keep your presence known to only those we feel must be informed. Canadian pride is an important, if not paramount, ingredient of current politics in this country."

"A very understandable reality," Holmes said.

"Your Mr Chamberlain, with whom I became more personally familiar during my recent visit to England, assures me that he and the marquis are keenly aware of the need for discretion and that, in London, the same care is being taken. But forgive me, gentlemen! We must not conduct our entire conversation in the hall."

With a disarming laugh, the Prime Minister turned towards the two or three domestics who stood deferentially at a discreet distance. In an instant, they had relieved us of our hats and coats.

"We have a few guests I would like you to meet." So saying, he showed Holmes and me through the large double doors into a spacious but tastefully decorated room.

"Ah, Zoe, my dear. May I present my wife. My dear, Mr Holmes and Dr Watson. Though they are, of necessity, travelling under assumed names, their objectives are only the loftiest. Gentlemen, my wife."

A fine-looking woman of mature years, Mrs Laurier exuded a quiet strength. The devotion existing between the couple was obvious. Holmes and I exchanged pleasantries with the gracious lady before turning to the other guests, who now stepped forward.

"Mr Clifford Sifton, Minister of the Interior." There was a forthrightness, confidence, and energy about the man that I immediately liked. He shook hands with exceptional vigour.

"Sifton is a Manitoban and exhibits the optimism of the region," Laurier added. "And recently, he visited the region in question with an official contingent, including Major Walsh, recently of the Mounted Police, and Mr William Ogilvie, our able surveyor who has been employed in determining the Alaskan-Yukon boundary, as you may know."

Beside Sifton stood a much older man who, at first glance, appeared almost frail. But as he fixed me with his keen gaze, wisdom and a great deal of experience were clear.

"May I present Sir Oliver Mowat, Justice. I coaxed him into federal service after a quarter century as Ontario Premier. I don't know if he's forgiven me yet, but we deeply value his wealth of experience. Really, Sir Oliver, I suppose you are, in fact, a Father of Confederation." Laurier turned towards the man warmly, who brushed aside the attention with a slight wave of his bony hand.

Holmes displayed his usual aplomb, and I trust that my own demeanour was appropriate to the circumstances. This might be the core of a colonial cabinet in a capital scarcely emerging from the wilderness, but these men seemed men of quality. The Prime Minister in particular exhibited a nobility of bearing that many an English peer might find daunting.

The dinner passed with pleasant conversation, Lady Laurier presiding with quiet efficiency as a few well-trained servants attended to the various courses. The lightly broiled trout was particularly succulent. Never did the Spey or the Dee provide better.

Retiring to the parlour pleasantly satiated, Holmes and the Prime Minister lost no time returning to the business that had brought us so many miles. Lady Laurier withdrew to leave the men to their tobacco, and Sir Oliver ensconced himself in a large chair by the fireplace. Sifton and I seated ourselves close by the two principals in this parley. A sense of common purpose and shared loyalties was exemplified in the large portrait of Her Imperial Majesty, a copy I believe of a Winterhalter. I assumed that its presence represented more than mere expediency on the part of this French Canadian with the impeccable manners and courtly style. One would have to be unduly cynical to believe that his acceptance of a knighthood from her beneficent hand had been simply an act of political opportunism.

"We Canadians walk a tightrope these days," said Laurier. "As a boy, I begged my father to take me to Niagara to see Blondin defy the falls. But now I have an even greater appreciation for his balancing act."

The Prime Minister placed a hand on the mantle and looked at us with a sly smile. The fire crackled gently, delivering welcome heat and a pleasant ruddy glow upon the room.

"The Americans seem intent on running off with half the globe these days. President McKinley clothes each new grab with high moral dressing, but the man whom I believe really poses the greatest threat is that new so-called hero of San Juan Hill. He apparently plans to parlay his luck into the New York governorship, but mark my word, that is only a stepping stone to much greater things. The truth of the matter is, it doesn't matter what job he holds, his bellicosity splashes over everywhere. You Englishmen will remember painfully how he enjoyed discomfiting London over Venezuela. I believe he does see himself as the strong hand of the Almighty. And that is the sort of peril we, in Canada, face these days—not just old-fashioned greed, but greed wrapped in virtuous platitudes."

One could sense the intensity of the Prime Minister's concern. Holmes drew thoughtfully on his pipe and nodded in concurrence.

"At the same time," the Prime Minister continued, "we Canadians recognize our historic ties to Great Britain—or at least the majority does. And we have watched the recent movement of your statesmen towards Anglo-American rapprochement. And where does that leave us, gentlemen? A very young and still small nation between two giants." Laurier's fist banged the mantle with a solid thud.

"Very true. Very true," Mowat concurred from the depth of his chair.

"Our commitment to the senior Dominion is total," I blurted.

"Well, we shall hope so. We shall hope so," said Sifton.

Holmes scowled and said nothing. Sir Oliver sat forward and, with a sigh, rearranged a log with the poker that stood on the hearth, causing a large shower of sparks.

"I do not intend to burden you with all the problems of the present Government; nor do I wish to restate the well known. As I have already said, your assistance is gratefully accepted by me and my colleagues," Laurier resumed. "That mischief makers from across the Atlantic are intent on working their havoc here should not, I suppose, come as a surprise. And I must tell you that, as a French Canadian, the Irish viewpoint is not beyond my understanding." With that, he raised his hand in a cautionary gesture.

I gripped my chair arm firmly and said nothing. Holmes was expressionless, his head wreathed in tobacco smoke.

"Please hear me out. I know I am treading on most delicate ground. This grand imperial enterprise, this dominion over palm and pine that London oversees with such high professions of good will and humanity has not been built without its costs. I do not have to tell you that I, myself, occupy a position between British authority and French Canadian aspirations and traditions that often leaves me at odds with both camps. If, for example, the empire goes to war against the Boers this year—and it does not seem unlikely—how shall I, as Prime Minister, deal with Canada's commitments to the Imperial Cabinet, while facing the outspoken and potentially violent opposition to this country's involvement in something French Canadians consider none of their affair?"

Laurier looked first at Holmes and then at me with a friendly but searching eye.

"And now London informs me of a plot afoot, apparently by Irish malcontents, to once more carry their age-old quarrel with the English to our shores. I will speak frankly and say that among a minority—let me stress it is a minority—of *habitant* descent, there is more than a little sympathy for the Irish republican cause. If fanatic Hibernians are even now in this country plotting evil for the Crown, we must deal effectively with them as lawbreakers, but we must remember that the emotional climate of the times does not simplify but complicates all our tasks."

Laurier folded his arms across his elegant frock coat and stood resolutely beside the fireplace, whose glow dramatized his features.

"We can, and we will, use the services of you gentlemen. Your evident capacity for incisive and effective action in foiling evildoers commends you to us. And this Government is not too proud to grasp a proffered hand when it is extended. But this project must be basically a Canadian affair. None of my countrymen—English or French—are in a mood these days to delegate their newly won sovereignty to others, no matter how beneficent or well intentioned those others may be."

"Understandable. Fully understandable," I muttered. Sir Oliver stirred the embers again and resumed his position of repose. Westminster chimes somewhere in a distant room sounded the quarter hour. Holmes had allowed his pipe to go out while giving his full attention to the refined figure before us, who spoke with such forthrightness and candour. Sir Wilfred would have cut an imposing figure in any European court.

"Lord Salisbury and Mr Chamberlain assure me that you are ready to proceed, fully recognizing these necessary constraints."

"Indeed we are," Holmes answered simply.

"I apologize for belabouring the point. I fear the pressures of the times are taking their toll. Even some of my most trusted friends now turn upon me." Laurier's words trailed off. For a moment, he stared into the glowing embers. "I fail as a host by appearing to whine. Forgive me, gentlemen."

The Prime Minister struck me as exceedingly tired. The rumour was about that once Laurier had left the heady atmosphere of the last imperial conference, he had regretted his emotional public utterances of commitment to Britannia in the more sombre atmosphere of Canadian realities. Even a man of this stature could be swept along on the currents of flattery, at which some of our leading countrymen are most adept. Now Holmes and I were in his country to assist him as we found possible, and he was trying to chart a course between colonial pride and limited Canadian resources.

"I am sorry that, of necessity, your services must remain unheralded and your sacrifices unrewarded. But I have already informed the Commissioner of the Northwest Mounted Police of your presence in the Dominion. You may count upon his cooperation and assistance, but I would not look for evidence of his gratitude."

"We do not look for gratitude, Prime Minister," Holmes responded. "We seek results."

"Don't misunderstand me. Commissioner Herchmer is a British patriot. He regularly expresses his readiness to serve the Empire to the far corners of the earth. I imagine he will be off to South Africa, should the worst happen there. But he and other prominent members of the Force believe that the NWMP is fully capable of handling any or all crimes, insurrections, or breaches of the peace that occur within our borders." Laurier paused again, momentarily lost in thought. "Perhaps he is correct. Their record in the West is impressive. But I am not averse to a bit of insurance. For that reason, London's offer of your services was gladly accepted."

"The force has made the West what it is," injected Sifton, who had been silent a very long time, listening carefully to the Prime Minister.

The Prime Minister now squared his shoulders and resumed his briefing.

"The man with whom you will find yourselves working most closely, however, is Sam Steele. Superintendent Samuel Benfield Steele, the officer in charge of the Dawson City Detachment of the Mounted Police. Steele is a man of integrity and flawless honesty, but his forceful character brooks little interference with his actions. Since his arrival in Dawson last June, he has become almost the personal embodiment of law and order. And with Dawson's population four-fifths American adventurers, that is no easy task."

"The Yanks have all but overrun the whole territory," chirped Sir Oliver from his nest. In the red glow of the firelight, he looked ancient indeed but wise.

"We are in the habit of cooperating actively with the police," said Holmes, with a faint smile that I imagine came from thoughts of the faithful Inspector Lestrade.

"All your undoubted gifts of diplomacy may be called for with Steele, but he is a good man and a top-notch servant of his country," Laurier stated with an air of finality.

Further discussion of the mission upon which we were embarking continued for some time, the Prime Minister demonstrating a remarkable mastery of matters within his own country and of the international situation as well. The sounding of midnight by that distant hall clock finally brought the engaging conversation to a halt.

The embers in the fireplace still cast a russet glow in the room. The aged Minister of Justice, for all his appearance of frailty had followed the conversation with avid attention, demonstrated by his infrequent but trenchant interjections. He now stood and vigorously shook hands with Holmes and myself. Sifton, too, extended a warm hand. The tinge of brusqueness in the westerner was to be expected I suppose. But he seemed a man of considerable talent and energy.

Mowat and Sifton took their leave, and Holmes and I were shown to our rooms on the second floor of the Laurier mansion.

"I trust that you will have a good night's rest. Your journey west will be lengthy but, I trust, comfortable," said our host as he stood at the lower landing. An efficient manservant informed us that our accommodations were all in order and our bags in place. I suddenly realized how weary I was. It had been a long day since we left Montreal.

CANADIAN PACIFIC

The railway coach into which Holmes and I climbed the next morning bore the name Mt Rundle. Our transcontinental journey was about to begin. Unlike our English trains, the carriage was not divided into compartments. The first class passengers we joined seemed a diverse but generally respectable lot. Carpets were clean and the antimacassars freshly laundered.

"The Canadian Pacific is putting its best foot forward," Holmes observed quietly as we settled into our seats.

"Quite civilized. Quite civilized I would say," said I. After a few tentative groans, our coach began its westward journey under protest. It seemed so very long since we had left Paddington Station, and yet we had not really begun our task. As if reading my thoughts, Holmes turned suddenly from the window.

"At last, doctor, I think we can safely say that it will not be long before we shall see some action."

"It still escapes me how we shall ferret out these blackguards in such a vast land," I said with a sudden sense of despair.

"The task becomes more manageable when one is reminded that we have a fair idea of their objective."

"But do they not have complete control over the choice of time and place?" I asked.

"That might seem so at first thought, but some careful reflection may perhaps reduce the odds against us. Villains of this sort select their vile deeds to create the maximum impact and generate the greatest shock and outrage. Now all we have to do is think with them about the circumstances and occasions that will best accomplish these deeds—to put ourselves in their shoes."

"Then too," I responded with some sense of relief, "we shall have the able services of Mr Cromwell Devlin, who strikes me as a well-informed chap."

Holmes seemed suddenly lost in thought, turning to gaze out the window at the passing landscape. Lush fields and meadows, exuberant in the full burst of spring, sped past. Their layout bore the imprint of English settlers. A Union Jack atop the flagpole by a small section crew hut snapped briskly in the breeze. A very tidy, though small, farmhouse also displayed our flag.

"Gratifying. Gratifying to see the evidences of Empire so proudly displayed," I said.

"UEL perhaps," Holmes added. "This is Loyalist country, built by those who could not countenance the American treachery."

"Yes. Yes. Likely Loyalist," I concurred.

In the distance that would have carried us from London to Manchester, we had yet to leave the pleasant farm land behind, though by late afternoon the evidences of habitation became more scattered.

Into the depths of the Canadian wilderness the train plunged. The endless click of the wheels punctuating the rhythmic sway and occasional lurch of our carriage mesmerized me and, I would judge, most of our fellow passengers. Long dark corridors of conifers relentlessly assailed the traveller's vision, broken briefly by a dark red railway shack or wooden water tower. A brief glimpse of silver, reflecting a nameless lake, pond, or swamp, punctuated the dark boreal curtain as a waxing moon rose. The yellow glow of the undulating lamps, which were now lighted, obscured the wild world without, but I could not but reflect on what a slender thread of civilization this track represented in the vastness of the cordillera.

"I suppose we should retire soon," Holmes finally suggested.

"Indeed," said I, "I think my evening repast is sufficiently digested for me to hazard the confines of that upper berth." "For railway cuisine, it was reasonably passable, do you not think?"

"By and large, yes," I answered, "though I notice we have been treated to stewed prunes both noon and night."

"Well, my good man," Holmes chuckled, "I believe these have come to be known as CPR strawberries. We probably have not seen the last of them."

Morning found us still amid the wilds of Nipigon. Even the vast expanses of the American plains I had crossed those years back on my way to San Francisco scarcely compared to the enormity of the wilderness miles that our train traversed north of Lake Superior. The glacier-scoured vastness of the Canadian Shield, with its endless array of lakes and forests, bore almost no sign of human habitation, except for the periodic water tower and railway service shack. The sun advanced steadily, overtook us, and left us behind as we rattled down the dark green forest corridors.

"The expanse of it all–the expanse," I exclaimed aloud.

"Westward the course of empire takes its way," Holmes responded idly. "I believe it was Berkeley, Bishop Berkeley, who said that, although he never had the privilege of this journey of ours."

"I beg your pardon, gentlemen. I could not help but overhear your exclamations regarding our vast country." The speaker was a Canadian of open and pleasant demeanour. His ready smile overcame my initial reticence at the intrusion.

"I suppose the enthusiasm that some of us show is simply a result of the newness of our country. Alongside your England, everything Canadian is only in barest infancy. But the promise of the future is great.

"Oh, excuse me, I have failed to introduce myself. My name is Bliss Carman."

Holmes also seemed drawn to the man, who stood swaying in the aisle by our seat as the carriage lurched 'round yet another of the interminable bends in the rail line that thrust its way westward, ever westward.

"Housman," said he, half rising and extending his hand. "And my colleague, Dr Wallace."

"I'm very happy to make your acquaintance. Perhaps you would join my travelling companion and myself in the dining car this evening. We are both, to say the least, enthusiastic friends of the Empire and value the British connection very dearly."

So it was that Holmes and I joined these two Canadians for the evening meal.

"Mr Housman, Dr Wallace, I would like you to meet Mr George Parkin," said Mr Carman as we approached their table.

Introductions completed, we satiated ourselves on Canadian Pacific cuisine, complete with stewed prunes, or should I call them "CPR strawberries."

"Geopolitics! That's the key," Parkin proclaimed as we settled into a final round of coffee. "I take what I call a world view of Canada. The British Empire is an integral whole, and Canada is a crucial part. And I must say, gentlemen, that this very railroad, this very line–the Canadian Pacific– is as critical a link in the geopolitical realities of the globe as ever was the Suez Canal or the Cape of Good Hope. Canada's future is also as a Pacific power, and the Dominion is essential to the maintenance of the Empire. As Sandford said so well, the CPR is the nervous system of the imperial organism."

"That would, of course, be Sandford Fleming," Holmes injected. "It is to him that we owe the rationalizing of international timekeeping, you will recall, Dr Wallace."

"Indeed. And on an journey of this proportion, time zones take on a significance that scarcely occurs to one in journeying from Thanet to Penzance," I replied.

"If I am not mistaken, I believe we are about to enter the Central time zone very shortly," Carman observed, drawing a fine gold timepiece from his waistcoat.

"What an incredible feat. To have forged an all-Canadian route into the west," I said, reflecting on the distances we had already come.

"Even if the Yank, van Horn, did mastermind it," Parkin added in brittle tone.

"Nonetheless, it is ours. A vital link but a fragile one," Carman responded, a deep frown creasing his forehead.

Parkin cleared his throat and brought his fist down rather forcefully on the table. "Would that I could share the optimism of the likes of Goldwin Smith about our American neighbours. Just look at this new outburst of American land-grabbing. Canada must defend itself. It will be a drain upon our resources, but to depend upon the restraint and goodwill of the Yankees would court disaster. Geopolitics! That's the key. We have to face reality."

Shortly taking leave of our new acquaintances, Holmes and I went directly to the sleeping car where a Negro porter efficiently prepared our berths.

"Canadian men of letters seem to share the same alarms that their politicians harbour," said I, "but Great Britain will not let them down."

"I hope you are right," Holmes replied, lofting his pillow with more vigour than seemed necessary.

Beyond the Lake of the Woods, I had a sense of change. We were entering the Canadian west. Manitoba seemed to exude a different atmosphere. Perhaps it was the two Indians (that is, of course, North American Indians) who boarded our train at a small hamlet called Rennie. I believe the Canadians refer to such places as whistle-stops. The Indians' arrival was noted by all the passengers in our carriage because the conductor had a difficult time persuading the aborigines that they were ticketed only for the colonist car, the appointments of which were, of course, distinctly inferior to those we enjoyed. I noted, however, a dignity and even a nobility about the man and his squaw, who received the berating of the railway official with stoic equanimity. Gathering their meagre bundles, one of which appeared to be a deer or elk skin bag, seriously mothor vermin-eaten, they marched in stately fashion to the back of our carriage and on to lesser facilities. A not unpleasant smell of wood smoke and leather assailed my nostrils as they passed.

"I cannot imagine a Sikh or a Hindoo behaving so decently," I observed. "I recall one occasion, I believe it was near Rawalpindi, when the conductor—"

But the train was gathering speed, and a prolonged blast of the engine's whistle drowned my words.

The railway tracks now extended westward in straight, determined lines. We sped along at an ever-increasing velocity, at times almost alarming. I had the distinct impression that even Holmes was somewhat anxious. Perhaps one could call it a premonition. Suddenly, there was a most violent lurch, and our carriage seemed momentarily airborne. A frightening splintering of wood mingled with the tortured twisting of steel and snapping of iron. I found myself flung to the floor with ghastly force. Covering my head with my arms, I closed my eyes and prepared for imminent departure from this life. A valise–I saw later what it was–struck me a painful blow in the lumbar region. Terrified human voices added to the cacophony. Had I survived the perils of Afghanistan, India, and my many adventures with Holmes to die in a train wreck on the Canadian prairies?

Then there was utter silence.

In a moment or two, I recognized the hiss of escaping steam and then a few moans and muffled voices. I opened my eyes and looked from under the seat beneath which I lay.

"Are you all right, Watson?" Holmes asked anxiously. He knelt in the aisle, a small cut in his forehead. The stress of the moment must have made him momentarily careless with my name.

"Yes. Yes … I think so," I said.

"There's been a derailment, but fortunately our carriage is still upright, and we appear to have survived," said my companion with a grin.

Now there were people stirring throughout our coach and the world seemed to have started rotating again after a moment's pause. The conductor came excitedly through the door, urging calm and reassuring us that all was well. One finely dressed woman had fainted, but the majority of the passengers that I could see seemed to have mastered their anxieties for the moment at least. The floor was littered with baggage of assorted sizes and shapes. I was, frankly, at a loss to see what all the rending of steel and wood had been. Aside from the disarray, the carriage itself seemed intact. In relatively orderly fashion, the passengers stumbled towards the doors.

"Careful now. Please, folks … wait till we can get a step for you. All is well. All is well," shouted the conductor. I believe he was trying to reassure himself.

The veneer of calm soon wore thin among us. Two or three men jumped to the ground, a distance of about five or six feet, as the carriage sat at a strange angle, not quite parallel to the rail bed.

"Women and children first. Women and children first," commanded the conductor. "Wait till we can get a ladder." These somewhat contradictory commands reminded me, in some bizarre way, of the lifeboat drills aboard the SS *Canada*. An element of farce was rapidly overtaking our situation. But before too many other male passengers had to risk a broken ankle or the females their dignity, someone from without produced a ladder, down which we were all able to descend.

Safely on solid ground beside the roadbed, I turned to survey the scene. We were, indeed, within a hair's breadth of catastrophe. Milling travellers stumbled past us with no evident sense of direction, seeking only to put distance between themselves and the conveyance they had trusted so unquestioningly, but which now sat in abject disorder.

"The travois never failed us like this," a voice stated in a sober matter-of-fact tone.

I turned to see the Indian and his squaw ascending the embankment behind us.

The conductor, now joined by a clerk from the baggage car, continued to shout alternate words of command and phrases of reassurance that helped no one, as far as I could see. It was now that I was reminded that the colonies were not England, for as I turned to Holmes and commented on the fact that the sleepers were torn up for a hundred yards, the conductor, overhearing me, became greatly agitated.

"Where, man, where?" he cried, a horrified expression on his face, alarm in his eyes.

I was at a loss to know the source of his new concern. "At ease," said Holmes. "I believe they are called ties, not sleepers, in the parlance of Canadian railway men. My colleague was merely observing that the ties along with the rails suffered extensive damage."

The conductor turned from us without further comment.

I would not burden the reader with the details of this incident, which appears to have no bearing on the purposes of our journey, except for the fact that it was in this fashion that Holmes and I came to make an unscheduled stop in Winnipeg.

The locomotive and several coaches had left the rails, but remarkably none had completely overturned. Ours lay canted precariously but in no apparent danger of further movement. That was not the case with two adjoining coaches, which hung over a small trestle. With surprising speed, would-be rescuers began to materialize. From a nearby village (I believe it bore the name Oakbank or Oakridge), a number of men arrived, together with the local constable and stationmaster. A number of what I took to be farm wagons soon assembled on a nearby road. Fortunately and, I might add, miraculously, injuries seemed to be minimal. Holmes and I assisted in the rescue of passengers from the nearby coaches, which was a tricky business, given the instability of their perch. I was able to render medical assistance to several whom had sustained minor contusions and abrasions. For the most part, it was a matter of reassuring and attempting to calm those who showed signs of extreme stress or panic.

Eventually, the immediate crisis having passed, Holmes and I tramped across the soggy field that separated us from the nearby road, accompanied by several locals. A goodly number of conveyances of an amazing variety had assembled there. A light rain had begun, and a chilling wind out of the north blew. We rode to the nearby hamlet in a bone-jarring rig called a buckboard. I must say it was well named. Nonetheless, we were thankful to have escaped this misadventure almost unscathed.

A representative of the railway assured us that we were only a few miles from Winnipeg and that carriages would be available soon to take us there, where the CPR would see to our needs and provide us accommodation until arrangements could be made to continue our journey.

"As long as their solicitations do not include stewed prunes, I think we shall be all right," I whispered to Holmes.

WINNIPEG

It was dark by the time we arrived in the city. But I was somewhat surprised by its apparent size. Here, after so many endless miles of wilderness and open land, was a community of creditable dimensions. As our carriage crossed the Red River, a blast of arctic air greeted us with startling suddenness. Although the calendar would have indicated that spring was well advanced, one would scarcely have guessed it by the intemperate surge.

"Wicked evening," said our driver, drawing more deeply into the folds of his massive mackintosh.

The street down which we now travelled was surprisingly broad.

"This here's Main Street, folks," he shouted to the passengers, in an attempt to cheer as much as to inform. "And the intersection yonder there is Portage Avenue. That there's said to be the coldest intersection in the British Empire." With that, he laughed uproariously.

I must say, these colonials had a unique sense of humour.

We were pleasantly surprised, however, by the hotel, before which we now stopped. The Fort Garry was an imposing edifice for this budding prairie town. The weary passengers, Holmes and myself included, showed evident relief at the prospect of a warm meal and a good bed after the harrowing experiences of the day. It was nearly midnight before Holmes and I were settled into our room, and sleep came almost immediately.

I was suddenly wrenched from the arms of Morpheus by a loud thump against the hallway door. Holmes was sitting upright in his bed, silhouetted before the window.

"What was that?" I mumbled, rising sleepily from the pillow.

"That's difficult to say, but we shall find out," Holmes replied, swinging his bony legs over the side of his bed and feeling for his slippers with his shiny white feet. Grabbing his robe, he crossed the room in large strides and flung the door open.

There, in the dimly lighted hall, lay a man clearly *in extremis*. A steadily growing dark stain spread concentrically from his torso across the hall carpet. Holmes bent close to the dying man's face. The stranger's lips moved weakly, but his words were too faint to be understood. I grasped his wrist, feeling only the weakest pulse. Clearly, there was no earthly help for the man.

Then, with agonizing effort, the prostrate victim drew his right hand across his blood-saturated chest and placed the palm with fingers fully extended upon the white wall by our door. With a rattling gasp, he expired, his right arm falling forlornly to the floor. I stood for a moment, transfixed with horror. The sight of blood and severe wounds becomes routine to one of my profession and lengthy experience, but the sudden and unexpected manner of this occasion left me numb. Holmes, too, seemed to be at a loss for the time being.

The silent moment ended with a high-pitched scream. Across the hall, a door opened and a matronly woman, awakened by the commotion outside her room, vented her alarm in the time-honoured fashion of the fair sex. Soon all doorways in the corridor were alive with gawking guests.

"Call the police," several yelled almost simultaneously. Immediately, the quiet that had marked our initial inspection of the unfortunate chap was replaced by a cacophony of panic, speculation, and indignation.

"Such things do not happen here," one guest pronounced.

"This is the Fort Garry—the finest, west of Toronto."

"Shameful, shameful," declared another guest in sepulchral tones that suggested he was a clergyman.

"Irish, obviously Irish," someone else observed. "Just about what one would expect."

This comment, though rude, did draw my attention to the luxuriant crop of red hair. Indeed, the dead man did look Irish. And for the first time since the horrible episode began, I was gripped with a gnawing awareness of the fact that this poor unfortunate might not have fallen against our door by sheer coincidence.

Holmes, catching my eye, seemed to convey the same unexpressed idea. But the arrival of an official of the hotel now quieted the gabble.

"I'm the night desk clerk," he announced. Seeing the inert form, the visage a ghastly white, he reeled backward and leaned on the wall. "Who is he? Not a guest surely? We are a quality establishment—a first class Canadian National hotel." The words tumbled forth from the poor man in an uncontrolled stream.

"Oh dear, he has made a mess of the carpet," injected the ample female who had first opened the door across the corridor.

"Scarcely the most important consideration right now," another bystander responded rather testily.

"Will you all please move back," Holmes ordered, rising from where he had been kneeling the whole time. "Nothing must be disturbed. The police have been summoned undoubtedly."

"Indeed they have, sir. Indeed they have," answered the clerk, now gaining some composure.

In a few minutes, two uniformed officers rushed into the corridor and descended upon the scene. The larger of the two, wearing sergeant's stripes and sporting a splendid set of snowy white mutton chops, immediately took control of the situation. He and the young constable with him took names, insisted that no one should leave without permission, and generally did an efficient job of determining that none of the guests had heard or seen anything until the unfortunate victim had stumbled against our door, waking Holmes and me.

I can assure the reader that giving our false names and identities to the Winnipeg police caused me no little internal turmoil. What sort of a world was this becoming when honourable gentlemen, with no nefarious purposes and only the loftiest of missions at hand, should be reduced to using such deceptions?

Soon, a full complement of peace officers, both uniformed and in civvies, arrived.

"These appear to be stab wounds, inflicted with a weapon of not less than eight or ten inches," stated one of the new arrivals, whom the sergeant deferred to respectfully. He appeared to be something of a forensics expert.

"The coroner," whispered Holmes. "The trembling hands suggest a washed-out and alcoholic surgeon whose nerves have failed."

The sergeant was concurring with the verdict of the kneeling examiner. "Yes, sir. I was thinking the same myself. A knife, and a big one at that," he nodded.

"He's staggered here from the back stairs. There's a trail of blood back there and down the stairs," another of the new arrivals called.

"Right, Inspector. He's come in from the alley and up these three flights. Remarkable! And hard to explain. What could he have wanted here?"

"Whatever it was, he made a superhuman effort to make it this far," said the man with the trembling hands.

"And neither of you have ever seen this man before?" asked the inspector suddenly turning to Holmes and me, his eyes narrowing menacingly.

"Indeed, we have not," answered Holmes looking him unblinkingly in the eye. "We have not the slightest idea who he is or where he comes from or why he should be so unfortunate as to fall mortally wounded before our door, awakening my colleague and myself from a much-needed sleep in the wake of the untoward circumstances of yesterday. I allude to the wreck on the Canadian Pacific mainline just east of here, which is the reason that the two of us are even in your fair city."

Holmes clearly believed that the best defence was a sharp offense. The inspector took a step backward and stroked his chin thoughtfully. He did not appear any brighter than poor Lestrade. By now, most of the hotel guests had been questioned and dismissed, and only the Winnipeg police remained beside the body.

Holmes was showing great restraint in not entering into the investigation with his most exceptional powers of observation and deduction. So far as the local officers were concerned, we were two newly arrived English gentlemen, briefly detoured from our cross-continental train trip.

Nonetheless, I noted that Holmes's keen eyes had not missed a single aspect of the gory scene. When at last the mortal remains of our nocturnal visitor were removed, Holmes and I reentered our room, assuring the police that we would be most happy to sign statements at the station house in the morning. Of course, there was nothing that we could add to what we had already stated. The first light of day was already evident through our window.

"The handprint on the wall—I can't get that final gesture out of my mind," I reflected as I climbed wearily back into bed. There seemed little likelihood of sleep now.

"Nor can I," said Holmes, as he rolled over with a sigh to face the wall.

Remarkably, I slept rather well, and the sun was close to its zenith when I opened my eyes. A brilliant shaft of light pierced the small gap in the drapes, and a cheery glow bathed the room, making the macabre events of the night seem illusory. Perhaps it had all been a bad dream. But stirring to full consciousness, I realized only too well how real it had all been. Holmes sat at the small desk, an intense scowl darkening his face. He was clearly lost in thought, and it was several moments before he seemed aware that I had awakened.

"Who could that unfortunate wretch have been?" I asked, knowing what was on my friend's mind.

"The fact that his pockets were empty and all means of identity were missing suggests that his assailant or assailants intended that no one should find out. Rest assured, he was no victim of mere strong-armed robbery or drunken assault."

"Was he coming to us? Was it no coincidence that it was to our door that he came?" This conviction was pressing itself upon me increasingly.

"Does a mortally wounded man climb three flights of stairs in a fashionable hotel for no reason in the middle of the night? One could scarcely mistake this for a hospital, no matter how confused or delirious he might be."

"Very true. Obviously true," I said, reflecting on the simple but powerful truth of Holmes's words. Coincidence was out of the question.

"Let us hope that the local authorities can be diverted from reaching the same conclusion, assuming that they have not already done so," said Holmes, rising to finish dressing. "We must do our duty now, filling out whatever forms the police have for us at the station. I trust our true identities can remain unknown. It would be an embarrassment, should Ottawa have to reveal our mission to the inspector and his colleagues. I don't know how enterprising the local press is, but the last thing we want is a headline in the local newspaper."

Fortunately, our visit to the police station did not produce any new questions that would have compromised our assumed identities. As far as the Winnipeg authorities were concerned, Mr Housman and Dr Wallace had been the occupants of the hotel room against whose door the unfortunate victim had fallen quite by chance. There was nothing to indicate the contrary, and Holmes and I were happy to leave it at that.

As we crossed the nicely appointed lobby of the Fort Garry, the desk clerk called out to Mr Housman.

"A gentleman to see you, sir. He's waiting over there beyond the potted palm."

We turned with some curiosity and headed in the direction the clerk pointed.

"Perhaps we'll have word on our railway bookings," I said. "The station master was most solicitous and promised every effort to be of assistance."

Further speculation was ended, however, as we rounded the greenery. There stood Cromwell Devlin.

"Gentlemen, on Her Majesty's Service, and at your service as well," he offered with a bow and a flourish of his hat.

"Well, sir, we had not expected to see you until we had reached the West Coast," said Holmes.

"Still, we are happy to see you now," I added.

"Well, when I learned of your misfortune on the rails, I thought it best if I came by to give you a hand. We mustn't have the local constabulary detaining you when you've other work to do," Devlin said with a smile.

"And how did you know of our misadventures?" asked Holmes.

"The derailment I learned of while making my own way west on the very line. I was but a day behind you. And when I set foot in this lobby a couple of hours back, the place was abuzz with tales of a dreadful crime committed hereabout in the middle of the night. Some were saying it was two English gentlemen who found the poor fellow gasping out his last in the hallway outside their door. Now tell me, was it not the two of you they're speaking of?"

He paused, tilting his head to one side. Taking a step closer, he dropped his voice even further, glancing about to make sure that there were no curious ears within hearing distance. "They're not going to detain you, are they?" he asked.

"I think not," said Holmes. "They seem well satisfied that we are but casual bystanders. And for that matter, I see no reason to think otherwise myself. Do you, Mr Devlin?"

"I wouldn't know, sir," Devlin replied, shrugging his shoulders in uncharacteristic modesty. "I hear the rumour that he was Irish. Did the man manage to say anything to you before he expired? One of the maids was telling a newspaperman that the poor fellow staggered in from the alley and up three flights of stairs—a giant effort that took. He must have been a bear of a man."

"He was a man of iron constitution no doubt," said Holmes, "but his collapse at our door hardly proves anything, other than that the human organism has limitations beyond which it cannot be pushed by any amount of will or determination."

"Did he gasp a name, a word, anything?" Devlin asked again.

"Not much that could be understood," Holmes replied.

"We heard nothing, only a ghastly death rattle," I injected, "but he did manage one curious thing. Just as he expired, the poor fellow drew his hand across his painfully wounded chest and reached for the wall, leaving a startling imprint of his hand in his own gore."

"That might well be a reflex of the nerves at the moment of death," Holmes suggested. "Is that not possible, doctor?"

"Yes, yes indeed. It might well be," I replied.

"And they say there was no identification on the poor man," said Devlin.

"You have surely gleaned the basic facts of the matter, Mr Devlin," Holmes stated with a narrow smile. "No doubt your experience with the Special Crimes Division stands you in good stead when it comes to establishing the pertinent information in a given case."

"It does, sir. And I have found that chambermaids usually know more than anyone else about the doings of a hotel, even a grand one like the Fort Garry."

At that moment, we were interrupted by one of the hotel boys with a message he extended to Holmes on a small silver plate.

"Message for Mr Housman, sirs. Desk clerk sent it over, sirs." The lad looked hopefully at the three of us.

"I'm Housman. Thank you, young man," said Holmes, fishing a coin from his waistcoat. "Ah, doctor, the CPR has seen fit to expedite our arrangements, and we can be on our way in the morning. And you, Mr Devlin, what are your plans?"

"I believe I shall be joining you. My trip to the West Coast seems permanently behind schedule now. But I am sure we can make up for lost time when we get to Vancouver. As they say, your wish is my command."

"Housman and I are grateful," I assured our companion.

As we returned to our room, workmen had just completed the laying of new carpeting in the hallway. The wall was freshly painted, and signs of the tragic events of the past night were gone.

"Winnipeg has held its surprises for us. I shall be happy to be on my way," said I.

Holmes smiled briefly. Then turning suddenly grave, he added, "I expect there are even greater surprises to come."

VANCOUVER

We both slept the sleep of exhaustion, scarcely stirring until a brisk knock at the door brought us back to consciousness.

"Mr Housman, Dr Wallace, six thirty. Your instructions last evening were to wake you now."

"Yes, thank you. Thank you very much," Holmes mumbled, already halfway to the floor.

"Come, my good man. Perhaps a quick breakfast before we board the train will preserve us from one extra helping of CPR strawberries."

It was with a sense of relief that I boarded the westbound train that forenoon. We had spent fewer than forty-eight hours in this budding prairie metropolis, but they had been harrowing hours in the extreme. I felt Holmes and I had come perilously close to being waylaid in pursuit of the mission we had come so far to accomplish. Cromwell Devlin seemed pleased to have rejoined us again. Holmes, too, seemed happy to be once more on the move. I rested my head against the freshly laundered antimacassar and dosed off in the warmth of the spring sunshine. Barring further derailments, we should see the Pacific within three days.

West of Winnipeg, the plains spread before and beside the rails in endless repetition, but colourful names such as Moosomin, Indian Head, Moose Jaw, and Medicine Hat enlivened the schedule. The territories of Assiniboia and Alberta each stretched further than the distance from Edinburgh to London. The great blue-grey barrier of the Rockies promised respite from the grassy sameness, though how this massive range was to be penetrated remained a mystery until the stout engines plunged into their elusive valleys. Adding locomotives to surmount the daunting grades, twisting torturously through stony gorges, threading across dizzying trestles, and plunging through figure eight tunnels blasted from the very bowels of the mountains, our train carried us day and night towards the Pacific. As the spectacular heights of the Fraser Canyon gave way to the lush green richness of the lower river valley, I could not help but feel a swelling pride in the energy and ingenuity of the Anglo-Saxon. Could any other people have carved this miracle through some of nature's most challenging terrain?

The mighty Fraser broadened and slowed, as if sensing its arduous journey was ending.

"Tidewater, I believe," said Holmes, leaning intently forward, his angular nose almost pressed against the window.

"What a journey it has been," said I, "and what a monument to engineering genius this Canadian Pacific is." "Yes, and built by an American at that," Devlin added, leaning across the aisle towards Holmes and myself. He stretched languidly and flashed a broad Gaelic smile.

"Port Moody, Port Moody next," announced the conductor, swaying rhythmically through the carriage.

"Port Moody in five minutes."

Unfolding the wrinkled railway schedule I had acquired in Winnipeg, I noted that we were just seven minutes behind our printed time of arrival.

"Half a continent and only seven minutes off target," I pointed out.

"And we shall be in Vancouver before the sun goes down," predicted Holmes.

Burrard Inlet could hardly have been more magnificent, bathed in the late afternoon sun, with the dark green of the conifers dipping to the waters and climbing steeply into the scattered low-lying clouds that hung above the opposite shore.

Vancouver was indeed a bustling seaport. The piers were piled with wares of every conceivable sort, while the harbour boasted vessels of every imaginable size and type—some, judging by appearance, none too seaworthy. On Cordoba Street, outfitters catering to the hoards of gold seekers who had come this way since '97 offered an unending variety of goods from socks, boots, and fur coats to mechanized placering equipment.

Charlatans were in abundance also. "Gentlemen," coaxed one bearded entrepreneur from the doorway of his cluttered establishment, "these spectacles are scientifically designed to reveal gold deposits as deep as thirty-five feet into the bowels of the earth—absolutely guaranteed."

"A superstitious fad of early frontier America," chuckled Holmes. "Treasure hunting was a popular obsession in New York State and such places."

Another very aggressive vendor actually caught my wrist. "Gentlemen, take salt with you. Salt. As much as you can manage. Did you know the ground is frozen just below the surface the year round where you're going?"

"The problem is real. The solution is futile," Holmes declared with amusement. We pushed on down the street.

A sign in one shop window caused me no little consternation. It read: "Help wanted. No English need apply."

"Good heavens, Holmes! Is this not British soil?" "Housman, man, Housman," came the reprimand in hushed tones.

"I suppose someday there will be a greater recognition that British and English are not exactly the same thing," he continued enigmatically.

Although Victoria and Seattle were far more important embarkation points for the Yukon, this fledgling seaport showed real signs of vigour and promising prospects for the future.

The crowds on wharves and nearby streets were impressive for so young and remote a town, though one stranger volunteered the information to Holmes and me that this was nothing to what it had been the past two years. I found this hard to believe, as the two of us were virtually immobilized amid the mass of humanity that jostled near Johnson and Kerfoot Klondike Outfitters. A well-informed and accommodating Englishman had recommended this establishment at our hotel, as a trustworthy and reputable firm, supplying the basic needs of the uninitiated Klondike traveller.

Unlike many of the businesses catering to the gold rush throngs, Johnston and Kerfoot did exude an air of permanence. Its stone-fronted exterior suggested stability, in contrast to many wooden-fronted shops, whose hasty erection or makeshift conversion testified to crass opportunism and exploitation of the unwary.

"Boom towns the world over quickly draw the same mixture of mankind," Holmes observed, as if reading my thoughts.

When finally we had obtained a modest but highly useful array of gear, we returned to our hotel, The Manor House. A note at the lobby desk informed us that Devlin was still seeking the quickest steamer passage north.

"Before we book passage, I want to make a few enquiries," said Holmes. "I have obtained a port authority listing of recent and forthcoming sailings for the goldfields. Perhaps we can narrow down the possibilities with respect to this 'Piper' of ours. As a nimrod stations himself where the buck must pass to stream or pond, so we shall watch for the quarry at this strategic locale."

"He may already be gone," I exclaimed, thinking of our antagonist's head start in London and our delay in Winnipeg.

"Perhaps forty-eight hours initially and an additional forty-eight en route, but our passage aboard the SS *Canada* must have recouped at least half of that. The vessel is one of the fastest in service." Now Holmes handed me the foolscap sheet he held in his hand. "You will observe that no passenger vessel or freighters carrying passengers has sailed in the last seventy-two hours."

"If we could just get our hands on him," I murmured. "If we could just get our hands on him, it would do us no good at all," Holmes replied. "To the present, he has broken no law, and even in England, no specific charge has been made. The Anglo-Saxon legal system we treasure so highly restrains us. Ours is not a tsarist tyranny where *agents provocateurs* and political police seize and imprison suspects on the frailest hint of calumny."

Still overwhelmed by the enormity of our task, I persisted. "This is a big town, and it's overrun with people."

"Yes, but we do know a few things that can help us narrow things down."

Holmes's penetrating eyes narrowed, and a faint smile crossed his lean face. So often, in those far-off, familiar surroundings on Baker Street, he had preceded a discourse on the science of deduction by such a look.

"What do we know about our quarry?" he asked quietly.

I glanced about the lobby. It was empty except for the desk clerk, who busied himself with a stack of papers, his green visor slightly askew and his black sleeve protectors the worse for wear. Holmes gestured towards two Morris chairs in the far corner, and we sat down. The rain had begun again, and Howe Street was awash. Only briefly, as our train had arrived last evening, had there been more than a hint of sunshine.

"What do we know about our quarry?" I repeated thoughtfully. "To begin with, we know the Piper is Irish, and probably his henchmen, which he surely must have, are also."

"That seems likely. As resourceful as he seems to be, he will probably have contacts and assistance—malcontents, Irish, and others."

"Wasn't it William Blake who said, if you would know the devil, find out his system?"

"And well said it was, Watson." Holmes himself, on occasion, forgot the pseudonym. "But what else can we say with assurance about out prey?"

"He's cold-blooded, a fanatic. He will stop at nothing." "Yes, yes. And what has driven him to this radicalism?" "He's Irish.... The whole history of our two islands—I suppose it's in his nature."

"Not nature but circumstances, doctor. He and his kind act as they do because they are powerless!"

"You are right, of course," I murmured. I had never quite thought of it that way before.

"If we think of Patrick the Piper not as evil but as a fairly ordinary fellow, who in other circumstances might be quite like you and I, it may be helpful."

"Surely, you're not suggesting that we are capable of such cowardly deeds–the death of innocent bystanders, the destruction of public property?"

"Come, come, doctor. Are you so certain? But never mind. It is probably better not to consider this proposition too long. My basic assumption is this–the Piper circulates with quite ordinary people, normally law-abiding."

"What are you saying?" I asked.

"I am saying, doctor, that we may be wrong to assume that we will find him among hardened and desperate men. The contacts and shelter he requires en route to his violent acts are likely to be found among quite ordinary people–expatriate Irish with only an abstract and romantic attachment to the cause."

"Yes, that seems likely," I nodded.

"While calling at the port authority, I also visited city hall, where I acquired a listing of clubs and saloons–shall we say social centres– frequented by large numbers of the sons of Erin in this city." Holmes patted his breast pocket.

"And?"

"And, with the assistance of a very helpful clerk who knows this city very well, I identified the most likely places where sympathizers might be found."

Holmes stood to his feet, surveying the spartan lobby of the hotel. Good accommodations were not easy to come by, the boom atmosphere still prevailing, but The Manor House was among the better. Two balconies and an ornate tower, at least, distinguished it from the many box-like structures that passed for lodging accommodations nearby. I had reason to believe that, before this journey was over, the present facilities would seem positively lavish.

"This evening, I shall visit the most promising," Holmes declared, heading to the stairway that led to our room above. "I suggest you find something to eat, while I make my preparations."

After a mediocre luncheon, which I ate in what passed for a Canadian restaurant, I returned to our hotel room to find Holmes seated before the mirror with makeup kit before him. As usual, the transformation that had taken place was quite uncanny.

"Is that really you, Holmes?" I laughed, forgetting myself again.

"Aye, it is lad," he replied with a lilting Irish brogue. The visage was the ruddy, coarse reflection of a windblown peasant of Galway or Mayo. Even the hands seemed to tell of the chiselling effects of sodden days of toil and depravation. The result was extraordinary. As he stood to his feet, he seemed several inches shorter, and any hint of his native Englishness was gone.

"Where in the world did you get those clothes?" I asked in amazement.

"One can obtain almost anything on Cordoba Street," he replied with evident satisfaction.

"You smell of mothballs," I observed light-heartedly.

"There are likely to be worse smells than that where I am going this evening," he grinned.

"And where, if I may be so bold, would that be?" I asked.

"You may, my friend," Holmes continued. Rarely had I seen him in such a jaunty mood. I supposed he was creating the character that he intended to assume, and like the consummate actor he was, he had already left the personality of the world's greatest consulting detective behind. I would have loved to see his Horatio on the London stage.[11]

"I have further refined my list of prospective gathering places. Three or four likely spots remain, but one has a particularly unsavoury reputation, if one can judge by the records of the local peacekeepers. Suspected Fenian expatriates are known to frequent it. And many of the less reputable of the Hibernians defy the rigid beverage laws of this province." The foregoing was delivered in an almost flawless Dublin accent.

"Well, for my money, you shall have no difficulty in passing for one of them. But these are dangerous men, and heaven help you if your subterfuge fails."

---

[11] According to Baring-Gould, Holmes appeared in *Hamlet* in October 1879. For a review of his theatrical career, see William S. Baring-Gould, *Sherlock Holmes of Baker Street* (New York: Bramhall House, 1962), 47–65.

"Your words of caution are noted and acknowledged," Holmes replied, suddenly grave.

"And what is the name of this place?" I asked.

"The name, I grant you, seems almost too obvious, but as we were saying a short time ago, the obvious is often overlooked for that very reason." Holmes smiled again. "It is called the Shamrock."

"Well, no one would accuse the proprietor of subtlety," I affirmed. "And just where is this place?"

"I'm afraid it is in one of the more disreputable sections of this city, which does not lack for disreputable quarters," Holmes admitted, "and for that reason, I shall need your assistance."

"I wish I could pass myself off as an Irishman, but I fear my English ways are too deeply ingrained, and my acting skills too limited to fool anyone," I confessed.

"Well, it is probably best that only one of us enter this leprechaun's lair anyway," said Holmes.

"What can I do then?" I asked.

"A change of clothing to make you less conspicuous." He pointed to some well-worn articles that lay on the chair by his bed. "Right down to some very badly scuffed boots. I hope I remembered your size correctly. I can't vouch for their cleanliness, but the shopkeeper assured me they had been sprayed for vermin."

"I scarcely know how—"

"Don't worry, this sartorial conglomeration will more than adequately disguise your professional bearing and prevent the most observant eyes from seeing a medical graduate of the University of London," he offered reassuringly.

The slightly wrinkled nankeens smelled musty as I picked them up to examine them. At least they looked intact, if somewhat threadbare. The flannel shirt was the sort that one saw everywhere along the waterfront. A tan ulster in reasonably good condition was to top my outfit.

"Try them on," Holmes ordered good-naturedly. "We shall see if clothes make the man. And don't forget the cap. It would hardly do for you to crown this haberdasher's nightmare with your elegant christy stiff."

"And in this attire, what am I to do?" I asked.

"You shall accompany me this evening and keep a sharp eye open for trouble. In the unlikely event that my disguise and my acting skills do not pass muster at the Shamrock, you must summon help from the local police. Report a riot, an altercation, a patron choking on tough mutton, a would-be suicide with a stick of dynamite—anything that conveys urgency and the need for speedy response."

"Good heavens! I would be hard-pressed not to rush personally to your aid from a band of angry Hibernians."

"I know, my friend. You have demonstrated your courage on many occasions, but it would be folly for both of us to tangle unaided with a ravening mob. The police keep a close watch on this part of town and are used to frequent and urgent demands for their assistance. At any rate, we will scout out the nearest source of help before we venture into this maw of Gaelic fanaticism. As for the rest of the afternoon, I suggest a good nap."

I found that I had little appetite for even the light evening repast that Holmes and I took at a nearby cafe. Holmes downed some overcooked kippers with apparent nonchalance, and I was relieved to see that our outlandish dress seemed to arouse no particular notice with either the dishevelled waitress or the somewhat seedy patrons. I spoke only guardedly and softly to Holmes, for fear that my accent would betray us, but Holmes was positively voluble, clearly testing the success of his disguise. It seemed we had passed the test.

It was growing dark when we entered Pender Street, having noted a nearby station house, where a gargantuan desk sergeant glowered over a massive but battered desk with all the imposing authority of a Queen's Bench Magistrate. I found his powerful presence, limelighted by a powerful incandescent lamp, reassuring.

"Lestrade could take a lesson in deportment from that one," Holmes observed whimsically.

Wood fire smoke drifted to us as we rounded the corner. A band of Indians had established an encampment along Alexander Street, testimony to the frontier atmosphere of this city.

The street on which the Shamrock was located was poorly fixed for streetlights, but numerous eateries and saloons emitted a fair amount of illumination. Mercifully, the day's steady rain had diminished to a mere drizzle. The sounds of accordions, fiddles, and penny whistles escaped from several of these shabby establishments, conveying an unmistakable Irish lilt. Sizeable numbers of men, some in advanced stages of inebriation, rambled down the street, while here and there the shrill sound of a woman's voice punctuated the general din of Gaelic sociability. It was clear that self-respecting females would avoid this labyrinth of nocturnal pleasures.

As we passed the brightly lit facade of one particularly festive parlour, a figure suddenly emerged from the deep shadows beyond. It was immediately familiar. With no little surprise, I recognized Cromwell Devlin.

In my astonishment, I nearly blurted his name, but a sharp poke from Holmes's elbow cut my exclamation short. Devlin passed us with only the briefest glance.

"Don't turn," Holmes whispered, continuing down the boardwalk without a second's break in his pace.

"What is Devlin doing here?" I queried half to myself. "Why should he not be here?" Holmes retorted. "He's an Irishman among Irishmen, and he's seeking the same scoundrels we are, is he not?"

"Well, yes, but I'll venture few of these down here would hesitate to slit an Orangeman's throat if they found him out."

"Perhaps equally an Englishman's," Holmes pronounced darkly.

His words sent a sudden chill through my frame. But now we spotted the Shamrock. The establishment had the appearance of a typical frontier saloon, complete with a rough wooden facade topped with elaborate wooden cornice fashioned by some colonial craftsman in a valiant attempt at aesthetic relief. One lone sign discretely read "Licensed Premises." Unlike the ribald atmosphere that marked similar structures on the street down which we had just come, the Shamrock seemed subdued and, to my thinking at least, almost ominous. No sound of revelry or unrestrained laughter met our ears from its doorway.

"Station yourself over there," Holmes said, pointing to a patch of deep shadows directly opposite the entry to the Shamrock's dimly lit interior. "I think you will be able to see enough of what goes on in there to determine if things are getting out of hand."

With that, he sauntered across the street and, without a moment's hesitation, pushed through the swinging doors. I was able to observe the interior by stepping onto a low tree stump that protruded beyond the wooden walk. The row of bedraggled geranium plants in assorted Empress Jam cans partially obstructed my view, but Holmes was visible enough. Within were a surprising number of patrons, considering the dearth of sound that was forthcoming. In one corner sat a diminutive figure, forlornly squeezing a small accordion. Several knots of men occupied tables and bar, exuding, it seemed to me, an air of earnestness rather than festivity. I frankly feared for my colleague's safety. My impulse was to find a policeman and report some catastrophe. But the sight of Holmes amiably leaning against the bar with a look of Gaelic nonchalance momentarily reassured me. I stepped down. As I waited in the darkness, the occasional figure passing along the street, generally too preoccupied with his own self-indulgence or too far gone in his bacchanalian pursuits to pay me any heed.

It seemed a long while that I stood there in the shadows, but upon striking a match to see my timepiece, I was surprised to see that less than a half hour had passed. A very brisk breeze now assailed me, and my patience began to wear thin. Once, a drunken reveller stumbled upon me with a start and hurled a string of garbled curses at me as he continued unsteadily down the street. Only the occasional patron passed through the doors of the Shamrock. Once, a paddy wagon appeared in the distance, and after a great deal of shouting and disturbance, several limp forms were bundled aboard.

At long last, Holmes emerged through the door I had watched so nervously, turned down the street, and walked off casually without so much as a glance in my direction. After a moment or two, I left my station and proceeded up the opposite side some fifty or so yards behind him. We continued in this fashion until we were far beyond the seedy environs of the Shamrock. I can tell you that I breathed a good deal easier as we put more distance between that neighbourhood and us.

Finally Holmes stopped, looked back towards me, and beckoned for me to join him.

"Well," he said cheerfully, "I hope you did not get yourself chilled while I enjoyed the warm conviviality of my countrymen. I learned some interesting things."

"That is good news," I replied, more cheerfully than I felt.

"Yes, but we must hurry. The rain is increasing, and I'm afraid I've subjected you rather needlessly to the elements this evening. My precautions proved quite unnecessary."

"I would have it no other way," I replied. "But you say you learned some interesting things. I'm surprised they would speak to a stranger, even if of their own sort."

"Oh, it's not that they spoke to me freely. It was rather a matter of observation and close attention to stray bits of conversation."

"Tell me more," said I impatiently. I knew Holmes could learn more by a sweeping survey of a crowded room than most people could in a week of close questioning and conversation.

"To begin with, the Shamrock was no ordinary saloon, devoted to nothing more than revelry and empty distractions. The crowd in there, I suppose, one might call intellectuals. At least they seem far from the carefree wastrels one normally finds in such places. That is not to say that they were all indifferent to the ordinary pleasures such establishments afford. Only, along with the more customary libations, many of the patrons seemed more than a little intoxicated with the heady wine of revolution."

"Good heavens, then your lead on the Shamrock was sound enough. How did you learn of it? I don't recall that you told me how you knew of it."

Holmes smiled broadly. His disguise was uncanny. He was every inch the Irishman he posed as. Yet his smile was unmistakable, as were his piercing eyes.

"The local police in fact. I simply told the inspector I was an English journalist doing an article for the *Illustrated London News* on immigration from the British Isles, and before he was through responding, he had denounced every Fenian sympathizer and assorted hothead in the city. Proud to be an S of E, he declared. And he invited me to the Sons of England Hall for the Saturday night social."

Holmes's evident amusement did not reduce the amazement I felt at this revelation.

"Do you mean to tell me that the Vancouver police know of the Shamrock's clientele and do nothing about it?" I gasped.

"Of course, doctor. Do you not expect the same proud traditions that offer shelter to anarchists, nihilists, and the like in our beloved homeland to prevail here also?"

"Yes, I suppose so, but ..."

"Then too, as the Inspector observed, what were a handful of crazed Irishmen alongside the surging tide of the yellow peril?" Holmes continued, his disapproval evident in his suddenly sober countenance.

"Did he say that? Did he really say that?"

"As a matter of fact, he did," Holmes nodded.

And for a few moments, we trudged along the dimly lit street in silence. Finally, he spoke.

"As far as the Shamrock is concerned, I would not doubt that at least one of the patrons was a police informer. I may have spotted him, but I am not entirely certain.

"I am convinced that Ottawa is not depending exclusively on us to foil the plotters. Nor did the Prime Minister ever suggest as much. Rumours abound of plots to seize the Yukon. The Canadians would be derelict in their duty if they failed to develop as many sources of intelligence as possible. I would not be surprised if one stood at the Shamrock bar with me this evening."

"But surely the revolutionaries are aware of the likelihood of such surveillance and are very close-mouthed," I observed.

"To a point, that is so. Yet there is a certain bravado that animates some—especially some Hibernians—who thoroughly enjoy the cat-and-mouse game with constituted authority."

We were now approaching our hotel, but the weariness that had overtaken me was suddenly dispelled by that same ubiquitous sign in another shop window: "Help wanted. No English need apply."

"Look a that!" I exclaimed, with renewed indignation.

"Prejudice finds many targets," Holmes replied soothingly. "We may better appreciate the anguish of those identified as the yellow peril. Even Englishmen are not liked by everyone."

I did not share my colleague's amusement, but we now stood at the hotel entrance. It was mute testimony to the unconventional and varied appearance of the frontier populace that our traverse of the lobby occasioned no particular attention. Such are the ways of the colonies.

In the dry warmth of our hotel room, I was anxious to hear what additional information Holmes had acquired. As we shed our damp togs, I pressed him to tell me more.

"There is one piece of information I picked up that may prove useful–the departure two days hence of a certain vessel for the north country, concerning which some of the Shamrock's patrons seemed inordinately interested."

"What is her name?" I asked.

"I'm afraid I missed that," Holmes confessed.

"But surely there must be many ships that may sail that day. How can we identify her?"

"This one should not prove to be too difficult to locate. She is carrying seventy-five horses on her deck, sheltered, I gather, with some sort of an awning. She is out of Seattle and has stopped here for repairs. From what I can gather, her captain would just as soon not have stopped here, but he had no choice. A stuck safety valve caused a boiler explosion that blew a small hole in her starboard side. She has been here for at least a fortnight, but she sails the day after tomorrow."

"But what has this vessel to do with the Shamrock radicals?"

"That, too, I do not know. But I do know that two of the Shamrock's patrons seemed intent on taking passage on her."

Holmes was now climbing into his bed. It was almost two in the morning, and I was suddenly aware of how tired I was. A steady rain had resumed, and it pelted noisily against the window as I opened the curtains and extinguished the lamp.

"Do you suppose—" I started, but my colleague's sonorous breathing told me my question would have to wait till morning.

Holmes had me up and about before it was properly daylight. After a hasty coffee, he hurried me towards the wharves. Mercifully, the rain had stopped, though a fine mist wafted from the inlet.

"Devlin should get my note when he checks at the desk this morning," Holmes said. "I asked him to meet us at the CPR depot at ten. By then, I hope we have located the ship in question. And we will be able to find out more about her."

"Devlin seems to have been doing considerable investigating on his own," I observed. "I wonder what he found out last night."

"Perhaps as much as we," Holmes replied.

"He is an enterprising chap. And he has rendered us valuable assistance since first we landed in this country," said I gratefully.

As Holmes had predicted, it was not too difficult for us to discover where the vessel in question was undergoing repairs. Inquiring at two or three repair works, we learned that a freighter answering the general description of the ship in question was just completing repairs at the Dominion Marine and Locomotive Yards, Ltd.

"We shall meet Devlin and then have a look at this craft," Holmes announced, glancing at his pocket watch. So saying, we set off for the railway depot that stood immediately by the grey waters of Burrard Inlet.

Devlin was waiting for us as we reached the entrance of the station. He greeted us with his usually cheerful Celtic buoyancy. One had to admire his perpetually high spirits, which seemed never dampened by weather or circumstances.

"Hello, my buckos. It's a fine bit of a brisk morning for ye, is it not?" he chirped. "I got your note at the desk, I did. And I hurried right down here to see what's happenin'."

"Good morning, Devlin," Holmes replied. "We've been looking around a bit since we last saw you, as I gather you have been also."

"Well, I have been trying to get a bit of a line on the troublemakers we're after," Devlin nodded.

"And have you picked up anything of value?" asked Holmes.

"Oh, a thing or two. The local coppers and the Mounties seem to be keeping as sharp an eye on the undesirables as they can. Of course, primary jurisdiction lies with the Vancouver police, but it doesn't keep the Force from nosing into things here about."

"Any sign of the Piper or his associates?" I asked.

"Well, yes and no. I've asked around, but those who might know aren't saying, and those who are inclined to talk probably don't know."

"Our quarry is not far off, I feel certain," I interjected.

"Quarry—noun, singular. But our problem is that the enemy is plural," said Holmes. "The British Empire would be destroyed by many foes in the name of many causes. We must avoid concentrating on one only while overlooking others as dangerous. So it will be worth our time to look at any potential threat. That is why we shall take time to visit the Dominion Marine Yards."

Holmes turned towards the line of horses and assorted carriages that awaited arriving train passengers and hailed the nearest of them. "The Dominion Marine and Locomotive Yards, please," he called.

Our information again proved correct. The ship in question was standing in the slip at the Dominion Yards. There was no mistaking her. Fresh signs of repair to her starboard hull forward of midship were evident. Her lines were far from graceful, but the ungainly canopy designed to shelter the horses would have caused a marine architect apoplexy. One rusting smokestack protruded aft of the grimy wheelhouse. It had been many a year since she had seen the business end of a paintbrush.

"So what's so special about this derelict?" asked Devlin as we wandered onto the wharf.

"It seems that some of your countrymen—of the wrong persuasion, of course—have a considerable interest in her. Just why, I'm not certain."

We turned towards a burly fellow, who ambled towards us from a nearby corrugated iron shed. "What do you want?" he growled. "Don't you see the barrier there? No admittance!"

"If I was to tell you that I am on official government business, would you moderate your tone?" snapped Holmes.

"What government business? You sound like a limey to me."

"This is the Queen's Dominion, and I can assure you that we are not idle sightseers. What can you tell me of that ship? Where is her crew and what is her destination?"

The authoritative tone Holmes had assumed seemed to inject some doubt into the fellow's dull self-assurance.

"What do you want to know for?" he asked somewhat more civilly.

"Perhaps you will be good enough to take me to the superintendent? He will be more cooperative, I am sure."

Our challenger took a step backwards and tugged at the rough woollen stocking cap that Canadians call a toque. His authority evaporating, he had clearly no desire to be caught in an act of insubordination.

"She's called the *President Polk*," he declared, clearly not certain of his grounds.

"Indeed," Holmes retorted, "but I can see that for myself. What else can you tell us?"

"She blew a boiler somewhere off Gabriola Island, I guess. Ancient tub. An old triple expansion engine. She's supposed to operate with an induced draft boiler at 125 pounds per square inch. Not much, as things go nowadays, but her at 125 pounds–no thanks!" The chap clearly intended to impress us with his technical mastery.

"A wonder no one was killed. Blew one bleeding horse overboard, but not a man with more than a singed beard. A wonder I tell you."

"Who are her owners?" Holmes asked. "Can't say. Don't know."

"Who is paying for the repairs?" Holmes continued. "The super could tell you that–if he had a mind to," the fellow answered with still a hint of belligerence.

The intense glare with which my associate fixed the man, however, seemed to make him a little more obliging.

"She's headed north with a survey crew or some engineers or something. I don't know. They seem a boisterous bunch, these Americans."

The fellow paused and glanced around the yard. No one seemed to be paying any attention to us. He stepped closer, assuming an air of confidentiality.

"You know there is one strange thing about this—"

"Yes," Holmes encouraged.

"This bunch seem pretty well armed for a survey party. Of course, there's a lot of grizzlies up there, but still ..."

"You are obviously an observant man–a man with his wits about him." Holmes tone was earnest.

The man looked self-consciously at his scuffed boots. The words clearly pleased him, a faint smile fleeing across his bristled face.

"Americans do like their guns, you know," he continued. "Canadians are more peaceful, eh? Like with the Indians. Tell you the truth, I don't much care for this bunch. Act like they own the place. Don't even give you the time of day." Clearly his indignation was rising as he spoke.

Devlin and I watched Holmes's performance with admiration. The man who had accosted us a few movements ago was now willing to confide all he knew about the *President Polk* and her crew.

"When does she sail?" Holmes asked.

"She's ready now. Repairs done. Scotch boiler ready to fire up. I guess she'll be on her way as soon as the customs men give their say so. She's been held in bond since they towed her in–nothing on, nothing off, except for exercising the horses that is." The fellow paused, a scowl now crossing his face.

"Some of these birds, though, they brag a lot. Talk too much, eh! Like Americans do. Mostly just talk. I don't pay much attention, but their gabbing can get you down."

Holmes seemed content to let the fellow ramble on. The sturdy oaf now seemed pleased to share his feelings.

"Arrogant pack. Boasting to a couple of Scotchmen how they were going to change the course of history."

"Scots did you say?" Holmes interrupted.

"Yes, right here. Yesterday."

"How did the Scots come to be here?"

"Oh, they came about noon, saying they wanted to see the captain. Said they had business with him. And while I was turning them away, Mr Westlake–the captain of this tub–hollers down that I'm to let them pass, that he has business with them."

"And you are sure they were Scots?"

"Of course I am. I see enough foreigners here, you know."

"Did they look like Scots?" Holmes persisted with a faint smile.

"Sure. They talked with a brogue, too."

"You can recognize a Scottish accent, can you?"

"Any day, man. Any day. Besides, I heard one say he was from Belfast."

"Oh yes, from Belfast. That settles it," Holmes concluded mildly. "Undoubtedly a Scot, if he's from Belfast."

Sarcasm is not one of Mr Holmes's nobler traits, but the look on his face almost caused me to burst out laughing. Devlin was struggling manfully to control himself.

"You mean they sounded like me," Devlin asked in his best Irish lilt.

"Yes, exactly. I know Scotch when I hear it."

"And this business about changing history–what was that?" Holmes continued.

"Well, the captain, Westlake, he wasn't happy with that talk. He tells his men–two of them were with him at the gangplank with these Scotchmen–he tells them to be quiet. He sees me standing by the shed there, and he doesn't look too happy. But I figure they're just gassing, the way Americans do."

"I see that you are indeed a patriot," Holmes continued, fixing the burly caretaker with a warm smile.

"I am. Born and raised right here. And proud of it." His jaw jutted out defiantly.

"Then as fellow patriots, perhaps you could arrange for us–my colleague, Dr Wallace, and myself–to look around that American ship."

"Oh no, I couldn't allow that. It's against regulations you know. And besides, there's always several of them Americans on board. Our customs men, they've been on her plenty. I guess everything is in good order." He shook his head vigorously, apparently appalled by the very suggestion that he should violate company policy.

"Well, certainly, no one would want you to anger your superiors. One has to go by the rules set down by those who put the bread on your table, so to speak," Holmes rejoined sympathetically.

"No, no. It's not that I'm not in charge here. Assistant yard supervisor, you know. I've looked after things here for years and never been second-guessed by the company. They trust me. I'm in charge."

"One can readily see that," said Holmes appreciatively. Taking the man by the arm and drawing him forward a step with an air of great confidentiality, he spoke with such guarded tones that I failed to catch what he was saying to the assistant supervisor. I glanced around the yards, half expecting to see some sinister figure lurking nearby, intent on overhearing the hushed and earnest words. But the yard was empty and totally still except for a wisp of wind that rustled the tall weeds that grew among the assorted winches, derricks, and scrap metal piles that lay rusting here and there. The *President Polk* strained at its mooring lines as the tide began to flow.

"Well maybe, maybe in this case. And since you are not just gawking sightseers.... Maybe we can arrange something. Frankly, I don't know what you think you are going to find that the customs men haven't already seen. It's a survey crew on the way to Alaska like I said."

"Yes you did Mr— I don't believe I caught the name," Holmes coaxed his newly won confidant.

"Wrong. Arthur Wrong," the assistant supervisor offered readily.

"And why, Mr Wrong, did two Irish–or rather Scotchmen–come looking for a survey crew from Puget Sound on its way to chart some coastal rain forest for some grasping speculator from south of the 49th parallel?" Holmes asked pointedly.

The man scratched his head, raised his bushy eyebrows, and said nothing. Slowly he turned, lost in thought, and beckoned us to follow.

"Maybe I'd better stay here," offered Devlin with unusual reticence. "Too many of us might make those boys nervous. I'll just have a seat here." The Irishman pointed to a large log by the shipyard fence, upon which the rare Vancouver sunshine was brightly shining for the moment.

"That might be just as well," Holmes nodded.

Avoiding the numerous puddles that dotted the yard, the three of us moved past the weathered shack. A battered wooden sign dangling from a single nail indicated that this was the shipyard office.

"Now if you're to board her, you'll need a reason. I suppose we could say—"

"Department of Health," Holmes interrupted. "Dr Wallace can certainly enquire into the status of the crew with respect to their vaccinations. Cholera and yellow fever are still rampant among vessels plying the Pacific particularly. And look! One of these mooring lines does not have a baffle to keep the rats from illegal entry." With a chuckle and evident enthusiasm, he strode towards the forlorn ship.

When we reached the gangplank, the wretched condition of the *President Polk* became more evident. Rust and neglect seemed to have had their way for so many years that scarcely a vestige of sound metal or wood could be seen. Her paint was almost nonexistent. Her wooden decks seemed almost too rotten to bear our weight as we stepped aboard.

"Permission to come aboard," Wrong shouted.

Crates stencilled APSC could been seen stacked none too neatly in the small forward hatch, whose cover lay carelessly amid assorted refuge, litter of lines, buckets, and barrels. One needed to be nimble to negotiate his way to the ladder leading to the bridge.

"What do you want?" A heavyset bearded man, wearing a threadbare naval jacket with bedraggled captain's bars and a captain's cap, rather the worse for wear, stood, feet planted apart with ham-like fists upon his hips, glaring at us with undisguised belligerence.

"Captain, sir. Captain Westlake. Two gentlemen from the Department of Health. Just a few questions for you, eh?"

"Department of Health? We're all fine here. Don't you government sorts ever get through? I thought we had a health inspector on board yesterday. In fact, I know we did. What's up?"

"Just a few moments of your time, Captain," Holmes injected, stepping up the ladder, undeterred by the captain's hostility. Nodding towards me, Holmes requested, or should I say demanded, that the captain show us assorted ship's papers and documents regarding the crew. "Dr Wallace will inspect these, verifying your compliance with the requirements of Canadian Maritime Health Regulations," he announced with an air that brooked no further discussion.

I trust my astonishment was not too apparent. I was totally unaware of the existence, far less the nature of, the assorted documents that my colleague so knowledgeably delineated. At any rate, the ruse seemed to work, for the captain led us aft from the bridge to his cabin with scarcely a murmur. As I stepped through the bulkhead, I received a nasty bump to my head. Overhead, a line of asbestos-covered pipes awaited the unwary. Westlake offered no apology for my discomfort. I suppose he considered it evidence of the landlubber's carelessness. Nonetheless, it seemed strange that the captain should endure such inconvenience, even on so miserable a vessel as this.

For the next half hour or so, I pored over the materials that the captain had brought to me, none too graciously I might add. Carrying out the charade to the best of my ability, I jotted notes, stroked my chin thoughtfully, and murmured appropriately. It appeared that the majority of the ship's complement was indeed comprised of surveyors. The rusting hulk was under lease to the Arctic Pacific Survey Company. I recalled the APSC stencils on various crates. Perhaps my colleagues' suspicions, for once, were unfounded.

While the captain was busily gathering the requested documents, Holmes absented himself on the pretext of inspecting potential health hazards. It was clear that the captain would like to have followed him, but he was too completely occupied with dredging up the documentation I was ostensibly examining. In a few minutes Holmes returned, escorted by a hulk of a man in oil-soaked dungarees.

"Cap'n. This here fella was nosing around below where he had no business being. Claims to be a health inspector. I asked him for some official proof that he's who he says he is, and he won't give me none."

The captain was suddenly highly discomfited. Alarm was written on his face. I could see that he had now realized his own careless failure to request evidence of the legitimacy of our mission in the face of Holmes's confident bravado.

"Say! Let me see your papers, buddy," he snarled at me.

"My medical credentials are entirely in order," said I indignantly.

"Sure, you may be a sawbones, all right, but where's your identification card or whatever from the Health Department?" he demanded, moving menacingly in my direction.

"Just a moment," Holmes commanded, placing himself firmly before the belligerent fellow. "You, and not we, are the ones called to account here. Your vessel is a profusion of hazards and infractions—a veritable floating coffin, a cesspool of filth. You will be cited under Articles xxvi and xxxi. Also, I've found clear violations of the Maritime Safety Act, Articles 18B and C. You may be quarantined indefinitely."

For a moment or two, I was not certain whether or not the captain and his sizeable cohort would resort to violence. Holmes had never shown greater coolness. As I have said elsewhere, the stage lost a fine actor when Sherlock Holmes became a specialist in crime. Neither man could quite decide how to deal with Holmes or myself. Holmes's bluff was so convincing that I, myself, felt almost indignant at the challenge to our official prerogatives. Even the caretaker who had brought us aboard and who, of course, knew of our pretence seemed to be swept along by Holmes's confident demeanour. He stood deferentially beside him, apparently ready to join in our defence.

At any rate, Holmes's bold front created a standoff that enabled us to leave the ship unimpeded. Captain Westlake was too unsure of his ground to take any strong measures or decisive action, and quickly, Holmes, the yardman, and I were down that gangplank and approaching the yard office.

"Thank you for your assistance," Holmes said, pausing before the office door and vigorously shaking Wrong's hand. The fellow grunted wordlessly and withdrew into the gloom of the shed. A satisfied smile crossed my friend's face as we retraced our steps across the yard to where Devlin waited.

"And did you learn anything worthwhile?" he asked as we approached.

"Several things," said Holmes, "several things."

"How did you persuade the chap to take us aboard?" I asked. The reversal of the man's earlier intransigence had amazed me. "Surely you struck a patriotic cord somewhere in his callused soul?"

"Not at all, my friend." Holmes chuckled. "I simply offered him a five-dollar bill, which I have just given him. Here in the colonies, filthy lucre is able to buy many things, even patriotic duty, I dare say."

"What can be better?" said Devlin. "Duty and profit at the same time."

"I must confess, this is all too cynical for me," I protested with a wave of my hand.

We were out of the yard and looking for a means of conveying ourselves back to Howe Street. Dark clouds again threatened.

"I think we can find an electric trolley a block or two that way," Holmes gestured as we turned up from the waterfront.

In the now grey dreariness of the Vancouver afternoon, a Chinese funeral procession curved its way down the street before us, a sad but picturesque testimony to the diversity that was making this new land. The sound of tinkling bells reached us on the rising breath of a chill wind, while paper ornaments and pastel banners flapped forlornly above the grieving Asiatics.

Shortly, a red car of the Vancouver Railway and Light Company swayed into view, and it was none too soon, for the rain had returned with a look of permanence to it. Once aboard, the three of us sat back to endure the noisy progress and rhythmic sway of our conveyance. Mud persisted everywhere.

"And did you learn anything aboard the *President Polk*?" asked Devlin, who sat facing Holmes and me.

"I did. And I confirmed my suspicions."

"And what was it you suspected?" he continued.

"That ship carried no ordinary survey crew. The captain's uneasiness at having to put in at this port is not surprising. Only good luck kept the Canadian officials from unearthing the truth about the *President Polk*."

"And what is that truth?" Devlin was indeed persistent.

"In my brief excursion below, before the very able-bodied seaman caught up with me, I discovered some hidden items of interest."

"Such as?" Devlin was on the edge of his seat.

"Such as several dismantled carts that might appear to be the ordinary cart a survey crew might employ, but which looked suspiciously like gun carriages–the sort that might carry small howitzers or Gatlings."

"Did you see any guns?" Devlin pressed.

"No," Holmes admitted with a faint smile. "But I know where they are."

"Come, man, where? How were they missed by the customs men?" I asked with growing excitement.

"I'll wager they are in the captain's cabin," said Holmes. "That ceiling, on which you received such a nasty blow, was quite unusually low. The moment we stepped through the bulkhead, I sensed the peculiarity of the cabin's dimensions. Even given the fact that maritime architecture often leaves little headroom, there was no reasonable explanation for the diminished height of the captain's quarters. Indeed, such quarters are likely to be the last place where sacrifices to minimal comfort are incorporated by the ship's designers."

"Assuming this vessel had such designers," I injected lightly.

"It was not that the ceiling was low, it was that the decking had been raised," Holmes continued.

"And beneath it, the clandestine pieces of ordnance," I gasped in amazement.

The trolley was filling now, and our conversation had to be suspended until we reached our Howe Street destination. A dash through the rain took us to the porch of The Manor House, where we shook the worst of the rain and mud from our coats, hats, and boots.

"Well, tell us more," I gasped as I caught my breath. "Who are these blackguards? And what are they up to?"

"We British might call them irregulars, or, to borrow from the Dutch, freebooters. I believe the preferred word these days among the Americans is filibusterer. The term derives from the Spanish, *filibustero*, a term, I fear, the Spanish have compelling reasons to understand very plainly, given their past experiences with Anglo-Saxons."

"Are you saying this band aboard the *President Polk* intends to seize the Yukon?" I asked.

"It would appear that the Alaska and Puget Sound Cavalry have nothing less in mind," Holmes replied.

"The Alaska and Puget Sound Cavalry! Who are they?"

Holmes paused with a mysterious smile. The rain was now torrential, and even in the shelter of the porch, we were getting wet.

"Gentlemen, shall we retreat to the lobby? I think we can find a private corner and avoid the worst of the elements."

Once we had hung our topcoats on the rack and placed our hats to dry on the nearby shelf, Holmes, Devlin, and I found three chairs discreetly distant from the other guests variously occupied in the lobby.

"The Alaska and Puget Sound Cavalry? How did you come by this information?" I asked again as Holmes drew his pipe from an inner pocket and proceeded to examine its bowl intently.

"APSC," Holmes murmured with deliberateness.

"Yes! Yes! I see. Arctic Pacific Survey. Alaska and Puget Sound Cavalry. APSC," I whispered breathlessly.

"The filibusterer is a dreamer, a romantic," Holmes continued. "He dreams of heroic deeds and triumphant moments of glory. He pursues a cause that he perceives as noble and even sacred. But his own ego is always an important part of what drives him."

"Like William Walker, the grey-eyed man of destiny," I injected, recalling the Tennessee adventurer of a generation ago in Central America.

"Or Leander Starr Jameson," Holmes added, citing a more recent—but English—example.

"What you're saying is that this is no innocent survey crew, but a renegade army," said Devlin.

"Yes. And one that intends to change history," Holmes affirmed, recalling the words overheard by shipyard attendant, Wrong.

Having now completed the packing of his pipe to his apparent satisfaction, Holmes felt his pockets for a match. Devlin handed him one, and the great detective now gave his full attention to lighting it. Soon, the heavy aromatic smoke curled around his head and, although many thousands of miles separated us from 221B Baker Street, I thought of the many hours we had spent so pleasantly there, I knew he would continue his dissertation when it suited him. Presently, he looked up.

"Convenient, wasn't it?" Holmes continued. "The Arctic Pacific Survey Company could provide a very useful cover for those dealing with Seattle port authorities, customs, and American maritime officers. But romantics can never resist the special touches that complete the pictures they have of themselves. And so it is with our Captain Westlake. He sees himself as far more than the master of an aged steamer. For him, duty is clear—to lead a band of patriots who will wrest the Yukon from John Bull and make it a part of the United States of America. And to that end he, and perhaps others with him, organized the Alaska and Puget Sound Cavalry. A bundle of saddle blankets stowed in the forward hatch were embroidered accordingly."

I can tell you, these revelations astounded me.

"I would wager that an inspection of the crew's quarters would reveal uniforms of some sort. Unfortunately, my investigations were cut short by the arrival of that oaf who insisted on taking me directly to the captain. I am confident, however, that he was not aware that I had already looked at the blankets. Had he or Westlake any idea that I had guessed the truth about the APSC, our safe departure from the *President Polk* might have been endangered."

Realizing the potential peril in which we had stood was sobering.

"This decides it then," I blurted in a barely retrained whisper, "we must notify the Canadian authorities. The whole bunch will have to be arrested and their nefarious schemes foiled right here. If we move with dispatch, perhaps they can be taken without any bloodshed."

"Not so fast, my good man," Holmes answered with a cautionary wave of his hand. "Whether Ottawa would welcome such an international incident at the moment is open to question. But a more compelling consideration may also commend itself."

"And what is that?" I asked.

"As you trained in surgery at St. Bartholomew's, did you ever encounter an abscessed appendix, doctor?"

"Of course, often," I answered, puzzled by the change of topic.

"And as a medical student, what was the indicated procedure?"

"A grave situation, indeed. Very touchy."

"Why would one not simply cut the morbidity out forthwith?"

"Peritonitis, man, peritonitis. The greatest danger in such a case would be that the offending matter would spread through the peritoneum. Then you have got trouble. Fatal. Almost always fatal. A first-year medical student would know the dangers of such a course of action." I shook my head in dismay.

"Exactly," said Holmes, "the ordinary layman might well know that also. And for that very reason, I think it best if we leave the Alaska and Puget Sound Cavalry alone for now. The poison may be contained, so to speak, if we refrain from the most drastic measures for the present."

"But—" I protested.

"Remember this, gentlemen; at the moment, we have located a centre of subversion and evil–Yankee adventurers and Irish fanatics, perhaps together in a plot of incalculable significance for the whole future of the North Pacific Coast and the interests of Her Britannic Majesty."

"You have a point there," I was forced to agree.

"So what do you propose?" asked Devlin, drumming impatiently with his right hand on the arm of his chair.

"I propose that we go to our rooms, wash up, and have a good dinner." Holmes stood up, tapped his pipe in the ashtray, and turned to retrieve his coat and hat. Devlin and I did the same. The rain showed no sign of letting up. The heat from the large coal stove in the centre of the lobby had almost dried mine.

"When the *President Polk* sails, we shall not be far behind, and I suspect that other like-minded enemies of the Crown and the Empire will not be far off," Holmes assured me as the two of us entered our room.

INSIDE PASSAGE

The *President Polk* sails at ten o'clock tonight," Holmes announced as I rinsed the soap form my shaving brush. It was a bright morning with no hint of the lowering clouds and rain that had prevailed since our arrival in Vancouver.

"You were about early this morning," said I. "You've put me to shame with your early rising. It was still dark when I heard you go out."

"Yes. Well, I wanted to check with the harbour master's office on ship traffic, and an obliging young clerk who was overseeing these things at such an uncivilized hour of the morning provided me just the information I sought." Holmes produced a paper, upon which he had copied a list of vessels' names and departure schedules.

"Fortunately for us, while the *President Polk* will depart before we can possibly find passage, she is a very slow vessel, capable of no more than five or six knots. I have already made enquiries about suitable transport for us, and I think we shall be confirmed aboard one of three ships that will head north in the next twenty-four to thirty-six hours. Any one of them will easily overtake the *Polk* and arrive at Skagway before our quarry does."

"If it arrives at all," I injected, only partly in jest. I towelled my face and placed my razor in its case.

"A point well taken," Holmes smiled.

The demand for northward passage had declined sharply in recent months. No longer was there an ever-swelling stream of humanity pressing hopefully and, often, mindlessly to the great Eldorado of the north. Argonauts; dreamers; confidence men, young and old; city dandies; and country bumpkins; high minded and low—all were older and wiser now. Some were very rich, but most no better off than before—and often worse. In this spring of 1899, reality was setting in, and for that reason, we found no difficulty in acquiring passage north.

"We are booked aboard the SS *Tartar*," Holmes informed me shortly after lunch. "She sails with the tide tomorrow."

"Tomorrow!" I exclaimed. "But the *President Polk*—"

"I told you, my dear chap, not to fear. The *Tartar* will overtake that ungainly hulk long before she clears the Queen Charlotte Straits. We may have a week's wait for her at Skagway, unless I miss my guess," Holmes assured me. "The *Tartar* was once a mailboat of the Cape Line, where more than one South African millionaire paced her decks."

"Well, she should be a pleasant enough craft then," I observed.

"I hope so," said Holmes with the shadow of a frown passing over his face. "It remains to be seen if she takes to these north Pacific waters as she did to the tropics."

Sombre skies and a steady deluge greeted us the following day. The pier where the *Tartar* was berthed was crowded with every description of mortal. Teamsters cursed drovers whose dumb beasts made progress along Water Street nearly impossible. A pigtailed Coolie with a handcart darted between lumbering drays, smart phaetons, and other conveyances, all reduced to immobility by the crush. The former's progress ended abruptly in a collision with a brightly painted rickshaw. The two Orientals were not slow to express their mutual disdain. Their exchange was lost, however, amid the curses, commands, and general din of unfamiliar accents and exotic tongues. I have rarely heard the scatological content of many of these vigorous exchanges matched, even in Soho Square or by the Billingsgate fishwives. A remarkable steam clock sounded the hour of ten with considerable whistling and belching of steam as we elbowed our way into the draughty plain wooden building that served as ship's terminal.

I am told that the situation was now much improved from what it had been the previous year, and it is my understanding that Victoria and Seattle were much worse. That being the case, I was sincerely thankful that our journey had been no earlier.

Aboard the *Tartar*, I was not encouraged. Whatever the amenities were in the vessel's prime, it had clearly now entered into an era of decay. Several voyages to the northland with a vastly overcrowded complement of passengers and a minimal crew, many of whom had abandoned ship upon reaching Skagway to seek their own fortunes, had left her in sad need of even the most routine maintenance. The cabin to which Holmes, Devlin, and I were assigned would have been scarcely adequate for two, but to our dismay, two additional passengers—neither of whom smelled the best—were already ensconced in the best of the original berths. To these were added makeshift bunks with straw mattresses and linens that may once have been white, but which long since had lost any pristine hue. Moving about in the cabin had to be, of necessity, a cooperative enterprise.

"Ain't nothing to what things was last season," offered the surly fellow who passed for a ship's steward. "They were in here like cordwood, them gold seekers. Like as not, most of 'em lost their shirts up there, and would be glad of a ride home on a cattle scow."

I refrained from mentioning that the implied distinction between cattle scow and the *Tartar* escaped me. It would not do to antagonize the fellow before our voyage had begun.

We did not have much time to assess our sorry accommodation, for we had barely seen to the storing of our gear, keeping only a small kit bag for use during the voyage, when the ship's horn sounded a great dissonant blast, and the mooring lines were dropped. As we slipped down the inlet and through the narrows, I counted the lifeboats. There seemed to be too few.

I will not burden the reader with a detailed account of our passage north, the likes of which I had not experienced before. Even my journey to India with the Fifth Northumberland did not rival this much shorter voyage for discomfort. I am not certain that the infernal heat of the Gulf of Suez could contribute as greatly to the store of human misery as did the raw winds and chilling waters of the British Columbian and Alaskan coasts. A dank and mildewed atmosphere permeated all interior spaces within the vessel. I have never been colder in my life.

Despite the shelter that the many coastal islands offered our route, the *Tartar*, at times, rolled and pitched in a most disconcerting fashion. Devlin did not look well for two or three days, spending long sullen sessions beating a rapid tattoo with his fingers upon the bunk rail, while Holmes seemed to endure the unpleasantness with stoic fortitude. I often felt somewhat queasy but managed to get the better of my discomfort by spending a lot of time along the ship's railing, lashed with wind and spray. All of this reduced one's appetite, which was just as well for the dining facilities and culinary fare left a great deal to be desired.

Nighttime was particularly trying, however, as the constant pounding of the ship's drive mechanisms made sleep almost impossible. We were informed that a flattened shaft was the source of our distress. Too much money was to be made by the vessel's owners for them to take it out of service. So an incessant thump marked each revolution with a deadening rhythm that threatened the sanity of any on board who were not otherwise anesthetized by strong drink. On occasion, our colleague, Devlin, seemed destined to join them, sharing a proffered bottle or jug with many a passenger, including the two strangers with whom we shared the cabin. I have never been a temperance advocate, but the bacchanalian frenzy of that voyage to Skagway remained a stern witness to the merits of moderation and sobriety. I was glad that Holmes had successfully conquered his unfortunate habit, for I had resolved that my modest store of medical supplies, hidden in my duffel, would be put to no unworthy purposes. Not for more than an hour in that entire dreadful journey did we catch so much as a glimpse of the sun. I feared, at times, that my very marrow would congeal.

At last, the *Tartar* entered the Taiya Inlet, narrowing from the Lynn Canal, the awesome blue-green immensity of the mountains embracing us in ever-tightening grip.

"Now the denouement of our task is at hand," exclaimed Holmes, eagerly scanning the grey waters beyond our bow for signs of human habitation. The fur cap, so incongruous on the London to Liverpool train, now seemed to suit his chiselled features admirably. The old glint was in his eye, the lethargy of the last few days now erased.

SK AGWAY

The first sighting of Skagway, however, was not encouraging. A pitiful collection of hovels lay in the distance, separated from us by a vast tidal flat across which enormously long but precarious appearing wooden piers snaked their way seaward. Gigantic tides and perilous currents turned this present element of the journey to Eldorado into a captain's nightmare.

"A year ago, you'd have got your feet wet from here," offered a veteran crewman, grinning brutishly at Holmes and me.

In a moment, he tossed a line to a waiting group of dockers who had ventured out to the end of one of those long skeletal structures. A brief surging reversal of the twin screws produced a green-grey mushroom of foam at the stern. With a dull thump, the rusting anchor disappeared into the dark swirling waters, accompanied by a jarring rattle of anchor chain. The *Tartar* strained at her fetters for a moment, threatening to tear loose the outermost pilings. But with diminishing groans and creaks, she seemed to accept her lot. The engines fell silent, to the immense relief of all, I am sure. For a moment, only the mournful sound of the frigid wind met our ears. I smiled at Holmes with a sigh of relief.

It is difficult to describe the squalor that greets the visitor to this entrepôt to Eldorado. Every conceivable sort of shelter from the elements could be seen with a sweep of the eye. The beach and mudflats were inundated with the sorry remnants of countless failed schemes and dashed expectations. Abandoned crates and battered packing cases, half-submerged hulks, and rusting machinery of obscure purpose lay in haphazard disarray. The town's muddy streets contained a varied representation of humanity, mostly male, together with dogs, assorted beasts of burden, wagons, and even a few velocipedes. And yet, amid this scene of primitive disorder, stood unmistakable signs of civilization and the quest for order and human progress. The gleaming, parallel strands of newly laid railway tracks could be seen rising above the habitations towards the cloud-covered pass. A freshly painted customs house stood prominently in midtown, an American flag briskly whipping in the wind.

"Be careful now," said Holmes, "this fellow, Soapy Smith,[12] may be dead, but his henchmen are undoubtedly about watching for a fresh bunch of unwary newcomers."

"Aye, there's bound to be two confidence men for every disembarking soul in this sinkhole of human depravity," Devlin added with a chuckle.

"Cheechakos, we are—but wary!" Holmes rejoined.

By some miracle, and in defiance of all the laws of probability, our entire compliment of baggage was retrieved, and we now struggled to deposit it safely at our hotel. The Golden North, as our domicile was named, was a small but glimmering relief from the numbing dreariness of the town's pathetic structures. Though only two stories high,[13] an effort at something resembling a byzantine dome crowned the front corner, conveying a brave effort at civilization. Its rooms seemed positively commodious after the long, cramped, and miserable nights aboard the *Tartar*. Prices for lodging and food in this mushrooming town were little short of extortionist. But our spirits improved rapidly as we ate—I think I might reasonably say devoured—a sumptuous baked salmon dinner.

"I wonder when we might expect the arrival of the *President Polk*," I asked, luxuriating in a third cup of coffee.

---

[12]   Jefferson Randolph Smith was a notorious con artist who virtually ran Skagway till his violent death. His followers, bunko artists and gangsters, were still a threat to the citizenry. His grave can still be seen in Skagway.

[13]   The structure was moved to its present location on Broadway and Third, and a third floor added shortly after Holmes and Watson were guests.

"I would judge that we will not see the Alaska and Puget Sound Cavalry for a day or two yet," Holmes responded, puffing thoughtfully on his black clay pipe.

Devlin was about to offer his own estimate of the situation when we were interrupted by a noisy commotion in the street directly outside our dining room window. Rising hurriedly from the table, we rushed outside with other equally curious guests. In the muddy roadway, two sizable gangs of men stood in bellicose confrontation.

"You thick-headed Canucks," yelled a barrel-chested ruffian from the front row of the nearer bunch. "Why don't you tell that fat old sow you call a queen that we claim the whole thing in the name of the United States of America." The last he drawled out in elongated phrasing, seeming to discover more syllables that one could have guessed were contained in the great republic's title.

"You bloody loudmouth Americans think you own everything, and everyone the world over is to bow and scrape to—" At that point, a missile hit the speaker full in the chest. As he staggered back, the air was filled with curses and vulgarity such as would be unthinkable to record for posterity.

Their respective cohorts now lustily joined both protagonists in a menacing advance towards each other. The melee that ensued was truly barbaric.

"'Tis a right proper donnybrook," exulted Devlin, who seemed anxious to join in. "Like the Whiteboys of Connaught."[14]

Holmes reached a restraining hand to him. "Discretion dictates that we stay well clear of this," Holmes cautioned with the trace of a smile.

"Did you hear that gross insult to Her Gracious Majesty?" I asked indignantly.

"And what would you expect from a gang of republicans?" Holmes calmly responded.

"Well, feelings run a mite high in this godforsaken hamlet," Devlin chuckled.

---

[14] The Whiteboys of Connaught was a secret society that harassed Irish landlords for their callousness towards tenant farmers.

"Yes, and we may turn that fact to our advantage shortly," said Holmes, his eyes narrowing to mere slits.

The thirst for combat finally satiated, the rival bands withdrew from the field of battle, and the spectators, like ourselves, returned to their respective concerns. Despite the late hour, it was still quite light out. The summer solstice was approaching, and in this northern latitude, there was scarcely such a thing as night.

The following morning, Holmes busied himself trying to locate the leader of the Canadians who had engaged in the previous evening's fracas, to what purpose he did not tell me. I wound my way through the primitive streets of the town, which were laid out in a rectangular grid on the narrow flats behind the tidal basin. The rails of the newly built railway ran down the centre of what might be called the main street. Someone had named it Broadway, in a burst of grandiloquence. It was, in fact, broader and less muddy than many lesser thoroughfares. A stout but modest log structure proclaimed itself the City Hall. Real estate offices were in no scarce supply. Drinking establishments were even more plentiful, adorned with such colourful names as the "Mangy Dog," the "Hungry Pup," and the "Home of Hooch."

It was, however, before a nameless enterprise conducting its business under a canvas roof and within rough timbered walls that I was fortunate enough to discover the object of Mr Holmes's search. The unmistakable Canadian accents that I had now learned to distinguish from the American counterpart caught my attention as I neared the back of town. A crude wooden sign simply said, "Drinks." Idling in the doorway, his right hand and arm swathed in dirty bandages, was one of last evening's most resolute pugilists. "Splendid show, last night. I was proud of the way you stood up for the Empire," I began, hoping to strike the right note of praise and cordiality.

The man looked quizzically at me for moment, apparently assessing my attire.

"English, eh?" he grunted. "Yeh, I guess we put in one for old Vicki. Well, God bless her and the Empire. That's what my old dad used to say. Three cheers for Victoria and the Empire. My dad was a limey, you know—came from a place called Upper Poppelton. Do you know it?"

I confessed that I did not but was pleased that the lad was proving somewhat convivial. Our words drew others out of the gloomy interior, and for several minutes, the exchange was animated. These Canadian boys struck me as solid patriots, less well bred and respectable than the sons of the English middle class, but a fresh and wholesome breed in contrast to the denizens of Whitechapel. As I returned to the Golden North, I felt certain that Holmes would be pleased with this initial contact.

"Indeed, I am," said Holmes, nodding approvingly as I told him of my visit to the outskirts of Skagway. "And I shall lose no time following up your efforts. I think we may have the means at hand to unmask the Alaska Pacific Survey Company for what it really is and to prevent their making mischief for the Crown in the Yukon." He did not explain further, but after placating our still ravenous appetites at the hotel dining room, he suggested that Devlin visit the waterfront to observe any new arrivals, while Holmes and I returned to chat with my newly made acquaintance.

The *President Polk* limped up the Taiya Inlet, a great rusting derelict. Her battered forward funnel spewed a dense cloud of smoke. She listed badly to port. And yet, among the assorted vessels that lay disconsolately about the harbour, she did not seem particularly worse than most. On the morning that Holmes and I walked to the moorage area, the sun had broken through and bathed the vista in splendid hues of dark green and blue.

With an asthmatic wheeze, the *President Polk* slid exhausted to its dock, emitting a last belch of smoke. A loud protest from pilings and groaning of cables reached our ears. The Alaska and Puget Sound Cavalry had arrived. How would Holmes foil their nefarious plans?

The remainder of the day we spent observing the debarkation procedures from a distance with field glasses–not that one would have found it difficult to approach the ship without notice, for the wharf was crowded with every sort and type of mankind. The unloading of the horses was not handled with great skill, but with remarkable good luck, the entire complement of those poor beasts was deposited on terra firma without major disaster. The wretched creatures looked as though they had not fared well on the long and trying journey north, but the cadaverous animals and grisly carcasses that greeted the eye everywhere ashore suggested the worst was yet to come for them.

"We have seen enough. They intend to camp over there towards the river," said Holmes, pointing across the flats to where a sparse copse of evergreens stood. With that, we left our station of the afternoon and headed back towards the hotel.

"They are making a good pretence of being a survey crew," Holmes reported as he returned from a mid-morning reconnaissance of the riverbank site. "Crates, duffel, wagons are being assembled, all conspicuously labelled 'APSC' or 'Alaska Pacific Survey Company.' They intend to pass innocently through Canadian customs en route to the Alaskan interior via the White Pass and the Yukon River." "Why do we not just inform the authorities and let them make their arrests or turn this band of blackguards back at the border?" I asked.

"Several factors must be taken into account, my dear fellow. To begin with, the Canadian authorities do not wish to create any incidents that would inflame the passions of their mighty neighbour. So, as stalwart and true as are the Northwest Mounted Police, our accusations might not be welcomed or taken too seriously at this stage. Then, too, American authority, which runs here despite strong claims to the contrary, is not likely to cooperate in embarrassing its own government by a serious investigation. And it is more likely that what passes for officialdom here is entirely sympathetic with such extralegal activities."

"By Jove," I exclaimed, "you have a point!"

"In fact, the Skagway citizenry in general seems rather fond of military posturing. I cite as evidence, doctor, the First Regiment, Alaskan National Guard. Company A was captained by one Jefferson Randolph Smith—"

"Soapy! Was that his name? Jefferson Randolph?" I asked.

"None other."

"He's about all we hear about since arriving in this lawless place."

"Yes. Jeff R Smith, patriotic founder of the Skagway Military Company as well, ready to lead his fellow citizens against those he styled the vile Spaniards who had allegedly sent the battleship *Maine* to the bottom of Havana harbour."

"What happened? Why did he not go to Cuba?"

"It seems the Secretary of War commended his patriotism but declined the offer."

"Better for him had he gone," I responded. "Dead this past year, at the hand of Frank Reid, the engineer who laid out the plan of this miserable town to his own enrichment and the impoverishment of others more deserving. At least, that is the tale I heard yesterday from the desk clerk." This idle talk I supposed Holmes had already heard. The ghost of Soapy Smith still lorded over the denizens of Skagway these months after his remains had been committed to the earth.

"Scoundrels and patriots," murmured Holmes, "scoundrels and patriots."

Now finished with our leisurely breakfast, I could restrain my curiosity no longer, and I asked Holmes to divulge his plans. With a patronizing grimace, Holmes glanced around the crowded dining room and suggested that we get a bit of fresh air now that the morning shower seemed to have passed.

As we walked up the primitive thoroughfare, so grandly designated Broadway, Holmes at last unfolded to me the essence of his intentions. And I will tell the reader in advance that the rashness, not to mention the almost criminal complexion, of the plan shook me more than a little. It was one thing to manage a small disturbance before Briony Lodge, as I have previously described in *A Scandal in Bohemia*, but it was quite another to contrive something akin to riot and insurrection. To such an unworthy level of conduct had the current practice of statecraft descended. The world's first and leading consulting detective had been reduced to conduct hardly worthy of a gentleman. Heaven help him if it failed and his role were to be exposed. Salisbury and Chamberlain would certainly disavow him.

Passing a modest structure that displayed a telegraph office sign in bright and neat letters, I suggested that we might be well advised to send a message to the outside, informing our superiors of our progress. Holmes laughed heartily.

"My dear doctor," he said with merriment, "I can see that you are a prime candidate for Mr Smith's confidence men. That late and unlamented Caesar must have had you in mind."

"I fail to see what is so funny," said I, a bit indignant. "Why, there are no lines leading from the office to anywhere!"

Holmes was right of course, as one could plainly realize with but a moment's reflection. Two strands of wire did extend behind the shed, but their terminal was undoubtedly in the small aspen grove at the back of the lot.

"But how?" I persisted, reflecting on the happy fellow I had seen yesterday, overjoyed with a cable verifying his sweetheart's undying faithfulness. "How can replies to outgoing messages—" The question died on my tongue.

"If one wants a reply, one can surely have one," Holmes said. "And in the case of the happy young swain we observed delighting in a message from home, why not make it the one he wanted to hear? Most of us hear what we want to anyway."

Early the next morning, the plan began to unfold. Harry Black, the self-appointed leader of the Canadian band from the edge of town, clamoured up the roof of the United States Customs House and lowered the American flag from its pole. With a flourish, he produced a sizable Union Jack from under his moth-eaten sweater, affixed it to the cord, and hoisted it into the wind with a triumphant shout.

"Long live the Queen!"

Two score or more voices echoed the refrain from the street below.

Customs officials exploded from the front door, looking up in alarm and confusion. Someone fired a rifle into the air with a deafening roar. Almost instantaneously, the curious and the concerned began to converge on the street.

"Get down from there, you fool," shouted an official in customs uniform, clearly not certain what was happening but incensed by the unauthorized clambering on his roof.

"I claim this inlet and the land adjacent to it in the name of Her Imperial Majesty, Victoria Regina," Black responded grandly.

Again there was a mighty cheer.

Skagway had seen its share of civil commotion in its brief history, but the atmosphere of riot that gripped it for the next few hours must have matched anything heretofore witnessed. The Canadians had carefully distributed their meagre numbers in a manner that gave the greatest possible impression of strength. No sooner was the disturbance at the Customs House properly ignited than another band contrived a wild head-bashing altercation with an assorted bunch of gold seekers recently arrived from New Orleans via Cape Horn. Some of the latter, being descendants of the Acadians, had no reason to avoid a skirmish with anyone loyal to things British. A great explosion off in the trees beyond town sounded very much like a howitzer being discharged (though in fact it was a medium keg of blasting powder recently pilfered from the White Pass and Yukon Railway). Rumour spread rapidly that the Royal Canadian Dragoons and the Royal Canadian Rifles were marching on the town. (In fact, both these forces had been merged with the Yukon Field Force the previous year and were nowhere near Skagway.)

Holmes and I observed this wave of pandemonium from the steep rocky slope to the east of the town site. I must confess my chagrin at the events unfolding before us, knowing as I did that my colleague was largely responsible for them. God forbid that there should be loss of life. The battle for the Customs House seemed more noisy than decisive. Fortunately, axe handles and fists appeared to be the most common weapon. Firearms seemed to be discharged in the air mostly for effect. Other minor skirmishes could be observed wherever Yanks and Canadians happened upon each other.

Rarely do Holmes's schemes and calculations misfire. But on this occasion, the intended results were not produced. Scanning the scene below through his field glasses, Holmes began to frown. "They've not taken the bait," he scowled. "More level-headed than I gave them credit for."

He handed me the binoculars. Focusing them on the camp of the Alaska and Puget Sound Cavalry, I could see a good deal of activity, but apparently Westlake had been clever enough not to expose his hand yet.

"One must never underestimate an opponent," I said. "Exactly," Holmes replied, "and perhaps I have been guilty of doing just that. Americans, especially westerners, may seem brash and primitive, but they should not be dismissed as simple bumpkins."

Holmes took the glasses and again surveyed the APSC campsite.

"No crates are being opened. They are not going to fall for our little game."

It seemed so. The Arctic Pacific Survey Company was only a civilian crew so far as local authorities were concerned. American officials in Skagway would not be embarrassed by any revelation to the contrary—at least today. The filibustering force seemed intent on retaining its cover for the time being. As I looked again through the glasses, I could see a sizable group of them grabbing up axe handles, assorted tree limbs, and stout slabs of lumber as they headed towards the fracas, but field pieces and rifles would apparently remain in the crates discreetly labelled APSC.

"A pity. A pity," Holmes murmured.

I lowered the glasses and looked at my friend. Keen disappointment etched his face.

"Ah well, it was worth a try," I offered.

"Foolish. I've been foolish. Never should I have taken this bunch so lightly," Holmes berated himself.

"But surely—" I began.

"No. No. I simply allowed some ungrounded prejudices to cloud my vision. It is inexcusable. I've endangered lives by falling prey to facile cleverness."

"My good man! I won't listen to you denounce yourself so," I countered firmly.

"Look at them! Bashing heads and bloodying noses down there." He surveyed the affray before the post office and the lesser skirmishes around the townsite below us.

"I hope there will be no fatalities," he said.

"Surely, the Canadians will withdraw as they see themselves outnumbered," I observed.

"Their retreat route and strategy was planned. Pray that it works. Those lads will soon be at a ten to one disadvantage. I hope their good sense overrides their courage and British ardour."

And so it seemed it would. For as Holmes spoke, the outnumbered ranks of the Canadians began to retreat towards the outskirts of town. Fisticuffs petered out. Here and there a fallen comrade was dragged from the scene. The curses and shouts declined. The odd discharge of a firearm punctuated the withdrawal, but the shots seemed to be aimed only at the sky. A light rain had begun, and everyone's enthusiasm for battle seemed to wane rapidly.

"We had best seek to be inconspicuous," said Holmes as we began to pick our way down from our vantage point. "American chauvinism will be at fever pitch in town after today's events."

A small group of Yanks had scrambled to the roof of the Customs House and was affixing a new flag to the pole. With a shout of triumph, they unfurled it. It was distressing to see the Union Jack tossed ignominiously to their compatriots below. A heavy mist had moved in from the inlet before we had slithered down the muddy trail that passed for a street. We were both, I believe, thankful for the anonymity it seemed to lend us as we returned to our hotel.

"I must fetch my bag and render what assistance I can to the Canadian boys," I whispered as we reached the vicinity of the recent battle. There was ample evidence that more than a few casualties had been sustained among the Americans, several of whom were being assisted painfully from the scene.

For the remainder of the evening, I tended to the contusions and traumas of some of those boys who had so bravely tackled the Yanks. I must say, however, that my conscience was far from clear as I reviewed the background of the recent violence and, alas, our role in it. I arrived exhausted at the Golden North and was asleep instantly.

The following morning dawned remarkably clear and sunny. The gloom of last evening, however, was evident on Holmes's face as he vigorously stropped this razor.

"We shall simply have to fall back on alternative means of foiling Westlake and his brigands," he announced as he saw me stirring into consciousness. "If the Americans cannot be made to contain their would-be filibusterers, then we shall have to find other means. And I am confident that such will be possible."

Rarely had I seen Holmes so despondent. I was truly thankful that he had successfully overcome his old habit. Both of us were relieved to learn, however, that there had been no fatalities in yesterday's encounters. Several men had required extensive stitches. There were some broken bones, but thankfully nothing worse than a compound fracture of the femur. The chief surgeon of the White Pass and Yukon Railway had been busy suturing wounds well into the night.

Harry Black, the erstwhile leader of the Canadian patriots, was incarcerated in the Skagway gaol, along with several others. This information we gleaned in the hotel dining room.

"There is, at least, one useful piece of intelligence that this late altercation had yielded," Holmes said in a low voice, as we finished a very expensive breakfast. "The Alaska National Guard of Soapy Smith's creation seems to have largely disintegrated. Nowhere yesterday was there any sign of military discipline or order among the locals. Street brawling will not wrest the Yukon from the Empire."

"Humm, yes, good. That is a bit reassuring," I concurred.

"That is not to say that military action against the Yukon is not yet possible," cautioned Holmes.

Our conversation lapsed as a burly waiter came none too graciously to enquire as to whether we were finished or not.

"The thing to remember," Holmes continued as we re-entered our room, "is that the threat is far more than military. Never forget for a moment that 'the Piper,' and undoubtedly others of his ilk, will stop at nothing to dislodge the good old flag. Who knows to what depth he will sink?"

My thoughts reverted to that afternoon so many months ago at the Travellers and to Lord Salisbury's ominous warnings.

"We seem stalemated here," Holmes continued gloomily. "We must continue into the Yukon and attempt to forestall 'the Piper,' as well as thwart the Puget Sound Cavalry, or any other adventurers who would threaten the British presence there."

"Will no one listen to us, Holmes? Cannot we warn Ottawa and have them lodge a protest with Washington?" I asked in exasperation.

"Warn them?" Holmes laughed. "Warn them of what? They already know the danger. And all protests will fall on deaf ears in Washington. Half the politicians there would be only too glad to aid and abet the entire project. If protests before the fact were capable of halting American expansionism—or Irish fanaticism for that matter—we could have saved ourselves an arduous trip. We could be enjoying, even now, the felicities of 221B Baker Street and Mrs Hudson's scones."

WHITE PASS AND YUKON

As we emerged onto the street before the Golden North, our attention was immediately turned towards the tidal flats and the lengthy wooden piers that reached precariously out towards deep water. It appeared that a sizable number of the citizenry was intent on greeting the newest arrival.

Devlin joined us with a cheerful greeting. He was, indeed, a chap of indomitable spirit.

"I shall rush on and see what the excitement is," he said.

"Certainly," said Holmes. "We shall follow shortly. A bit of a walk will be bracing."

As Devlin bolted off, I drew my collar closely around my neck. A chill wind reached up from the sea. I thought Holmes's spirits somewhat restored in the forty-eight hours since the skirmish with its unhappy results.

"We shall waste no more time in Skagway," Holmes announced with determination. "I shall have Devlin see to our baggage and supplies. We must be off as quickly as possible for the Yukon."

The tracks of the White Pass and Yukon line ran down the centre of the street in front of us and off towards the lofty backdrop of mountains. Looking at them again renewed my concern.

"Yes," said Holmes, sensing my thoughts, "we shall, I hope, be fortunate enough to start this portion of our travel in greater comfort than was even imaginable a few months ago. How we complete it may be another matter!"

"I am sure we will be up to whatever the challenges may be," I replied.

"If we are lucky, the sturdy little locomotive will carry us over the White Pass with much less labour than so many thousands expended in making that journey in the recent past. Rumour has it that the rails will reach Lake Bennett by midsummer," he continued.

"That will be splendid," said I.

"Rumour also has it that service is notoriously unpredictable," he added.

"Yes," I chuckled, remembering a comment I had heard in the hotel. "They say the initials really mean 'Wait Patiently and You'll Ride.'"

Reaching the piers and the milling crowd, we spotted Devlin.

"That is the *George W. Elder*," the Irishman informed us.

"She's a trim ship," I said with admiration. The vessel stood as a swan among the mudlarks.

"And so she should be, as the vessel of the Harriman Expedition."

"I'm sorry, I haven't heard of it," I admitted.

"A prime example of capitalist benefaction, the advancement of scientific knowledge, or vulgar exhibitionism," Devlin replied light-heartedly. "Mr Harriman, of Union Pacific fame, it seems, has brought a grand collection of scientists and naturalists and high mucky-mucks to view the great north, which, no doubt, he hopes will all fall into his hands–for the benefit of the American people, of course."

"Most interesting," said Holmes, beckoning us in the direction of a large group of passengers who had just disembarked from the ship in question. "If I am not mistaken, that lean fellow with the black beard is John Muir, the conservationist."

"Conservationist?" I asked.

"Yes, a very new and ardent cause for the Americans–the preservation of nature and the end to spoliation of the earth. And if this fellow, Roosevelt, should receive the presidential nomination next year, the cause will acquire a sacred aura."

"A railway baron and a champion of wilderness–strange bedfellows," Devlin added.

I mention the arrival of the *George W. Elder* because its party came to play a brief role in our adventure. Through it, we were able to avoid the customary delays forecast for passengers of the White Pass and Yukon line. The morning after the ship's arrival, a smiling Holmes announced that we were to leave immediately for the train as he had secured an invitation to ride to the summit of the White Pass with the Harriman party, who were guests of the railway. The hour was early considering the time that we had retired the night before, but the opportunity was not to be missed of course. So in a steady drizzle, we boarded the narrow gauge carriage after seeing to the sizable mound of baggage that our trip to Dawson still required.

Introduced to Edward Harriman as Dr Wallace, I felt a mild twinge of conscience at our deceit. The millionaire seemed happy enough to make our acquaintance, despite the recent unpleasantness between his countrymen and the Canadians, about which he had undoubtedly heard. Not everyone in his party was as gracious as he, but Holmes displayed his most charming side, and the civilities of the hour were accomplished well enough.

"I should like you to meet Mr Muir," said Harriman, as the lean and angular naturalist joined us in the forward carriage.

"A great pleasure," said Holmes with a crisp bow. "Your reputation has reached far–even to the isles from which you come."

Stroking his ample beard, Muir exchanged pleasantries with us, though we were forced to sit down rather quickly on the nearest seat, as the train suddenly lurched into motion. Harriman laughed. The railway baron–or railroad baron, as the North Americans say–was as subject to the vagaries of the "iron horse" as any of us.

The train laboured along the recently laid tracks, passing quickly beyond the simple log cabins comprising the outskirts of Skagway. Visibility improved momentarily, and all the passengers strained towards the windows to get a glimpse of these environs made famous, or notorious, to the far reaches of the globe. Before long, the pace slackened as the engine began to toil up the increasingly precipitous grade beyond the town. Heavy smoke belched from the funnel, momentarily obscuring the view, but the landscape unfolding before us was increasingly daunting.

"Porcupine Hill," announced the railway conductor as he swayed down the aisle. "Killed more horses, and, yes, even men, than any similar stretch of trail from Skagway to Dawson."

Indeed, the stark remains of pack animals and other debris were still visible as our ascent continued. The almost luxurious nature of our journey, in contrast to that of the gold seekers of only a year ago, was truly remarkable. The remains of one poor beast could be seen by the trail below, its four legs extended rigidly, like some overturned piece of rough furniture. Whitening skulls and rib cages, still draped in decaying strips of hide, defiled the terrain. The view suggested the emptying of some giant charnel house.

"I fear the events of the last few years have dealt harshly with Muir's precious wilderness," observed Harriman as he gazed reflectively at the unfolding scene materializing and dissolving in the fog before our windows.

"How easily men trade the cleansing purity of a spruce forest for the sordid squalor of a gold camp," Muir murmured.

"Ah, progress. Progress has its price. None of us welcomes the ravaging of nature, but change must come." Harriman's countenance seemed to show genuine regret.

"And what brings the three of you to Skagway and the Yukon?" The enquiry came from Mrs Harriman, who had finally herded the smaller of her two young boys into a seat by her husband.

With a shriek of delight, the lad pointed to yet another grisly carcass splayed out pathetically on a rocky defile.

Devlin's mouth opened, but Holmes seized the moment. "I suppose one might say that my associates and I are simply fulfilling individual cases of wanderlust," said he with a winning smile. He handed the young Harriman a horehound drop.

"Mr Devlin on occasion reports for the Belfast *Gazette*, while Dr Wallace has suspended his Harley Street practice for the time being to accompany me to the Klondike to study social deviance in a frontier environment. I have, in the past, made extensive study of criminal behaviour in Whitechapel and East London in general."

I feared Holmes's story was merging closer to the truth than was wise. It might not take much for so perceptive an observer as Harriman to penetrate the Housman guise and identify the world's leading detective.

"Then you are, in fact, a scholar," Mrs Harriman responded.

"Alas, more properly, only a student. A student of people. Particularly, those who defy the conventions that society–rightly or wrongly–finds necessary to assure order and stability."

"I understand that order and stability very nearly broke down in Skagway in the last few days," said Harriman.

The conversation was again verging on the perilous.

"A most unfortunate thing," Holmes nodded, "that two such closely related communities should descend to violence."

Holmes clicked his tongue disapprovingly. I felt a flush of guilt as I thought of our role in those events.

"Civilized men should be able to settle their differences without resort to violence," pronounced Harriman. "This boundary business should not cause any great or lasting discord. The English are reasonable men, and so are we."

"But what of the Canadians?" I blurted. "Is not this their—"

"Power. Power is what counts. And this matter is simply a routine question of power politics," Harriman interrupted.

"This trivial dispute should not be allowed to poison relations between two great powers."

"Trivial, maybe," injected Devlin with a grin, "but whose flag is it that's flyin' over that miserable hamlet down there?"

The twinkle in the Irishman's eye and the jovial manner of his words prevented any of the Americans from taking offense. The vista that passed before the window was awe-inspiring. Bottomless gorges and thrusting granite crags alternated through the infrequent gaps in the lowering mists and clouds.

John Muir, who had been staring intently out his window, turned now to our conversation. "It is a pity that in this whole affair, neither England nor America nor Canada will be the ultimate loser. Nature and the wilderness will be the final victim."

This sobering thought was delivered as the little engine gave a series of rapid gasps and the grade slackened. We were approaching the summit of White Pass. Though the tracks stretched on to Lake Bennett, we had reached the limit of the service now available on the White Pass and Yukon line. With a final hiss, the locomotive halted, its heroic labours done for this day.

The Harriman party noisily and excitedly disembarked and we with them. The immediate impression upon me was one of utter desolation. Rarely do I recall so bleak a landscape. The clouds pressed in upon the summit, dark and ominous. That the sun still shone above them seemed hard to believe. A chilling wind almost took my breath away as I took the long step down to the few boards that served as a platform. The dampness of the air made me suddenly aware of my old wound. Some tenacious but pitiful spruce and subalpine fir trees thrust through the grey expanse of rock and retreating snow.

Numerous puddles, ponds, and small lakes dotted the weather-scoured landscape. An endless array of icy streams flowed between them. Such meadows as existed between rocky outcroppings consisted of spongy, bog-like ground, dotted with cotton grass, arctic rose, and fireweed.

A rather pathetic collection of tents and primitive huts—if one could describe the random assembly of boards and planks as such—could be seen from the summit. The scene did not gladden the heart, I can tell you.

Two lean flagpoles adorned the summit with a well-weathered Union Jack flapping noisily from one, while the other boasted nothing more than a remnant of the Stars and Stripes. How the tents averted being swept to their destruction by the incessant gale was difficult to see. Despite the inhospitable character of the scene, however, the sight of our flag moved me. The Empire indeed did reach to the far-flung corners of the globe.

The party members were, by now, dispersing. Mr Muir expressed his best wishes to us and strode off purposefully to enjoy the wild vistas he so cherished. The scientific members appeared anxious to gather specimens of flora and fauna, as tenuous as was their existence. With various instruments, others took readings and recorded data. The Harriman family began towards a collection of tents huddling by a solitary log cabin. The little boys cavorted enthusiastically among the boulders, seemingly oblivious to the harsh conditions.

Holmes, Devlin, and I saw to our supplies, which seemed even more mountainous now than in Skagway, and definitely more cumbersome than when we'd first assembled them in Vancouver.

"You would think the Yanks could at least afford a flag," I commented, looking at the tattered rag that continued to shred itself with every snap.

"I believe it represents a protest," said Holmes. "It would seem that the government of the United States refuses even to acknowledge this boundary. Their contention is that the line actually stands twelve miles east of here," Holmes replied.

"But the Canadians are here, and that's what counts," said Devlin, as he deposited the last of our gear on the ground.

As he spoke, a blue-uniformed Canadian officer approached us.

"Good day, gentlemen," he said with authority.

"Good day, sir," responded Holmes, straightening his lean frame as he stepped from among the duffel and assorted cases.

Upon hearing the English accent, the officer's demeanour seemed to change. He looked puzzled.

"I thought you were with the Harriman party," he stated half apologetically.

"Indeed, they were good enough to allow us to share the train, but we are travelling independently of them," Holmes explained.

"English. British subject then?"

Holmes nodded, reaching for his papers.

"Well, I shall not have to create more unhappiness today then," the man responded with a broad grin. "I'm afraid I've made a lot of travellers quite unhappy. I'm required to collect customs duties on all goods imported by Americans. They don't take kindly to it. I must say, one fellow yesterday seemed ready to declare war personally."

"Let us hope it does not come to that," I replied fervently.

Most of the Harriman party had, by now, reached the tent town. The officer, who seemed pleased he was not obliged to face any unpleasantness with us, quickly cleared our supplies. Surveying our inventory, he asserted that we were in conformity with the laws requiring all parties heading for the gold fields to have sufficient provisions to ensure survival. The wisdom of such requirements seemed self-evident, as I thought of the journey ahead.

Thanking him warmly for expediting our return to British soil, we headed towards the encampment to bid the Harrimans a goodbye and thank them for their generous help in expediting our trip from Skagway to the White Pass summit. To my amazement, the smell of the most savoury cooking wafted on the wind as we approached the cluster of canvas structures. To our immense pleasure, we were invited to join the entire group in a remarkably sumptuous feast that had been provided by the officials of the White Pass and Yukon. Clearly, their desire was to impress the railway magnate and his company. As I enjoyed a last piece of meringue pie, I reflected on the fact that, in all likelihood, our palates would not taste anything like this for a very long time.

"We must see to our provisions," Holmes said, as the luncheon party began to drift away from the now less-burdened tables. "We should have no difficulty in obtaining a string of packhorses. Demand has declined, and I am told we can very nearly name our price."

"A fellow from Lake Bennett has already offered me an animal, but the poor beast had the blind staggers," said Devlin with a chuckle. "The rogue thought he had a gullible Irishman to hoodwink."

"Cheechakos had better beware!" Holmes nodded.

By mid-afternoon, the Harriman party was preparing to return to the train, whose engine was again building a head of steam and belching great clouds of black smoke into the ever-present wind. The three of us hastened to thank our host for his graciousness. Soon, the noisy throng had retreated to the waiting carriages, and the festive atmosphere had dissipated. The pitiful huddle of tent-cabins that made up White Pass

City was suddenly very melancholy. Skagway now seemed the height of civilized amenities when compared to this place.

I will confess to a certain elation when, the next morning, we started the trip to Lake Bennett. Holmes had obtained three scrawny packhorses at a still sizable fee from the one remaining ostler in the community. Sleep had been nigh impossible through the night, as the wind had driven every shred of canvas in this tent town to a maxim gun staccato.

The trail—for it was certainly no road—to Lake Bennett was a rutted, miserable series of mud holes and rocks along which we struggled endlessly. The ease with which we had ascended the White Pass by rail had temporarily lulled us into a false impression of the journey ahead. We were completely exhausted by the time we reached the sprawling collection of tents, huts, and hovels that comprised the community. The wild disarray was even more startling than that of either White Pass City or Skagway. Without rhyme or reason, canvas roofs were strewn around the curving banks of the lake, which stretched grey to the northern horizon.

To my great relief, we quickly located an abandoned cabin, which conveniently offered enough sparse forage for our beasts of burden. I did not recall lying down on the crude bunk on which I found myself in the morning. When I awoke, to my great surprise, the sun was shining. It was Holmes's voice from the doorway that roused me to full consciousness.

"They appear to have made remarkable time," he said. "Who?" I asked.

"The Alaska and Puget Sound Cavalry," he replied, shifting his lean frame awkwardly back through the doorway, which was a good foot shorter than he. "Or should I say the Arctic Pacific Survey Company?"

Devlin, who had extracted himself from the corner bunk with luxuriant groans, stumbled to the door to peer into the bright exterior.

"Bejabers!" he muttered, tapping a rapid beat with his fingers on the rough doorframe.

There was no mistaking it. As I thrust my head out the cabin entrance, the glare contrasting to the gloom of the interior was almost overpowering. But as my eyes adjusted to the brilliance and the landscape focused for me, there was no mistaking the string of horses and the row of tents assembled not fifty yards from our domicile.

"The NWMP did not penetrate their disguise," I said, turning to my colleague, who busied himself with the coffeepot and assorted tins of provender.

"Do you not concur in the tired cliché about giving a man enough rope?" Holmes smiled.

"You really do mean to make no effort to have them apprehended then?" I asked. "Would it not be better to stymie these rogues here and now, at the frontier, than to allow them to march right into the heart of Her Majesty's territory?"

"One could, of course, turn them back so that they might regroup, reinforce their numbers, and seek some alternative method or route of entry. Who knows how many ways they might find to still accomplish their goals when their first plan of action, their first strategy failed them?" Holmes paused, seeming to review his thinking on the subject, and nodded confidently.

The wind was biting, and I drew back from the entrance to seek the meagre warmth that the small stove emitted. The coffee that Holmes now poured steaming into the enamel cups seemed almost a lifesaver.

"Never fear, my good man, we shall not recklessly endanger our cause by underestimating the ingenuity of the foe. But if we draw him a little further onto our grounds, we shall be able to deal with him once and for all with the sort of finality that I know you will appreciate."

Again Holmes seemed momentarily lost in thought—perhaps rechecking his calculations. He looked fleetingly at Devlin then turned his gaze on me. Was there a hint of uncertainty in those steely, penetrating eyes?

"I had half expected that this band of amateur troopers would have turned back, aware that the game was up and their charade unmasked."

Long ago I had learned to leave my colleague to his innermost thought processes at such times as this.

"How would they guess that their guise was penetrated?" asked Devlin.

Holmes did not reply but picked up the mug of coffee he had poured for himself.

"Enamel cups are for the devil," exclaimed Devlin, having too quickly lifted his to his lips.

"They have the one redeeming feature of being unbreakable," said Holmes, carefully blowing the edge of his, steam mingling with his own breath in the chill atmosphere of the cabin.

I must say I have been more comfortable facing a northern gale at John O'Groats than inside this miserable shack, even with its stove and its cheesecloth-covered windows. I suppressed the urge to ask Holmes what he had in mind for the filibusters. I knew he would divulge his schemes at the right time and place.

Devlin, who was struggling with the ingredients of a great staple of the trail, sourdough pancakes, apparently also recognized that Holmes should be left to his own thoughts. Pouring the pasty mixture onto the griddle, he seemed lost in his own thoughts, and for once, he had nothing to say.

By the time we were reasonably victualled, the sunlight that had greeted us was gone, replaced by the sombre clouds that dominated this land. Our first task of the day was to be rid of our pack animals; the second, to locate some sort of a watercraft to continue our journey to Eldorado. Within an hour, we had sold our horses to an ostler whose partner at White Pass City had provided the broken-down creatures at an exorbitant price. The man drove a hard bargain, and Holmes seemed to be in no mood to quibble. We were clearly not in a strong bargaining position.

Finding a seaworthy boat was a more daunting task. We recognized that we were ill-prepared to begin the hazardous passage of the lake and the even more hazardous descent of the Yukon River with its fabled rapids, falls, and whirlpools. Holmes and I had little experience in such endeavours, and Devlin admitted to an equally serious void, coupled with a fear of drowning. What a man endures for Queen and Country! What one endures for Empire!

A less promising array of crafts could scarcely be imagined. Crude planking, ribbing timber, masts and spars had been fashioned in countless saw pits, where countless gold seekers had, for the past two or three years, laboured in purgatorial conditions to expedite their final journey to Dawson and Klondike fields. The granite-faced giant who offered us a craft that I would hardly have cared to board for a Sunday cruise on the Serpentine did not reassure me. We were mercifully rescued from this towering confidence man by the arrival of a member of the Northwest Mounted Police.

"Build them long and build them strong," the tall and youthful Corporal boomed out as he slithered down the embankment to the lake shore where we stood forlornly surveying the pathetic piece of marine architecture being peddled by this Goliath.

"This thing is caulked with newspaper soaked in spruce gum and about as seaworthy as a laundry tub," the Mountie chuckled as he joined us on the muddy bank.

With a pleasant smile but an air of authority, he addressed the craft's owner. "Evans, when are you going to stop sending good men to their doom in these boats of yours? How often must I remind you that all vessels must be inspected and assigned an identification number before they are permitted to begin the Yukon voyage?"

Without waiting for an answer, the Corporal turned again to us. "Gentlemen, I think I can offer you alternative and safer transport. In fact, I have been instructed"–with this he drew closer to Holmes and myself and assumed an air of confidentiality, speaking in a very low voice–"by my superiors, and I mean my superiors, to render you every service possible."

"Well that is splendid," said I with relief. "Thank you," Holmes responded heartily.

"I don't believe these gentlemen will be needing your services, Evans. Thank you." The Corporal touched the brim of his hat to the scowling Welshman. "And remember, all vessels are to be inspected and numbered."

As we followed the policeman back up the bank, Evans threw a curse in our direction, but all of us chose to ignore it.

"One makes a living as he can, I suppose," reflected Devlin, lightheartedly scrambling through the ooze.

"I'm not certain just who you are, but Ogilvie himself sends word to render Housman, Wallace, and those accompanying them every assistance. Yes, those very words–'to render every assistance.'"

"Ogilvie?" I asked.

"Ogilvie himself," the Corporal repeated. "William Ogilvie, Commissioner of the Yukon. None other! And Steele says to step lively. And Pennyquick tells me, and here I am." The young man laughed heartily.

"Steele? Pennyquick?"

"Forgive me. I talk too fast–and too much, I am told. Pennyquick's my Sar—"

"That would be Samuel Steele, Inspector–or should I say Superintendent–of the Force in the Yukon," Holmes said, ignoring the Corporal's apology.

"Yes, sir. Right you are, sir. Oh, I'm sorry. My name is Pipes. Corporal Pipes at your service."

"Well, Corporal Pipes, we thank you," Holmes said with a wry smile.

"And since it appears that you are needing a boat of some sort, I have just the thing to suggest–a small cutter that the Force has available."

It was clear that the Mountie was duly impressed with our importance, from whatever source his orders had come. But Pipes naive buoyancy did not conform to the expected demeanour of a member of the Force that had, in the quarter century since its founding, become almost legendary. Observing the Corporal and his scarlet tunic, it occurred to me that the NWMP was, indeed, a unique organization– half army, half police. These men were the stuff of myth.

And was not our Empire here, as in India or Africa, in part a magnificent facade, hiding some shabby quarters like the false fronts of those gaudy drinking establishments in Skagway? I supposed this gloomy thought burst upon me because of the disquieting sight of miserable Indian encampments and dispirited Athabaskans that we had seen during our journey downriver. However great the present bonanza might be, not all were to share it even partially. This momentary retreat from my usual optimism came as a surprise. Pipes's cheerful call broke my reverie, and I resolved to suppress such thoughts in the future.

With enthusiasm, he led us, slithering and sliding, along the sandy shoreline to where the vessel lay moored. The cutter, while it could have used a fresh coat of paint, seemed reassuringly solid. Even a glance distinguished it from the average craft that cluttered the bank and shallows. Unlike the great majority, it clearly appeared to have been more than the design and workmanship of an amateur. Our continuing trip to Dawson looked instantly more promising.

DOWNRIVER

The wilderness waters through which we now passed, while having an awe-inspiring beauty, were so unpredictable and potentially savage that the unwary traveller might well forfeit his life with a moment's negligence. The most sturdy vessel would be tested to the full crossing Lake Bennett, not to mention the surging rapids and treacherous eddies of the Yukon.

"Make them long and make them strong. That's what we tell them," Pipes declared, cheerfully pointing to the skeletal remains of several craft that had proved to be neither. "Make them long and strong. The Yukon is both!" (Young Pipes had a way of repeating himself.)

The small sawmill at Lake Bennett, which now stood almost idle, clearly had been a busy place in recent seasons, offering for a price a merciful alternative to the saw pits.

"Many a lifelong friendship ended right in those saw pits," the ever-cheerful Corporal asserted. "That little sawmill was nothing but a stream-driven gold mine last year."

The sudden and savage winds of the lakes provided their tense moments, but they were, to me, as nothing compared to the awesome power and primeval violence of the Yukon's rapids. This river proved to be every bit as formidable as we had been told it was. I shall never forget how, time and again, the distant dull roar warned of yet another cataract, quickening the pulse and honing the senses. As our craft shot forward at ever-increasing speed, the cacophony of torrential waters, swirling winds, and groaning planking assaulted my every nerve. The basalt cliffs seemed to edge ever closer as they sped by with alarming velocity. At such a time, a sidelong glance at Holmes revealed that sharply chiselled profile, with chin set resolutely and eyes fixed in utter concentration upon the course of our craft by boulders and whirlpools, any one of which could have destroyed us in an instant.

The Miles Canyon rapids swallowed us in a green and white maelstrom of rock and water, toyed with us as pitiable Lilliputians in a land of giants, and spewed us forth with total indifference. The perpendicular walls of hexagonally shaped basalt reminded me of Fingal's Cave. Damp and exhausted, we found ourselves in an eerie silence. But our experiences there were to be surpassed by an even more gargantuan display of nature's wrath in the White Horse rapids. Words fail to express the sheer terror of that descent. Even Holmes seemed robbed of his aplomb during that experience. No sooner had we crested one enormous wave to begin the fearsome plunge into the trough than a still more towering wall of liquid destruction threatened to dash us and our insignificant craft to oblivion. But in some manner, and thanks to Corporal Pipes's considerable skill, we emerged more or less intact.

"Superintendent Steele tightened the regulations here," Pipes commented with a smile as we complimented him on his boatmanship. "More than 150 boats went down here in '98—before the Super imposed regulations on crafts and helmsmen. Truth is, no one but an utter fool would even run these rapids if he had a good look at them first."

The Corporal clearly enjoyed the wonder that he had inspired in the three of us.

After the White Horse rapids, the trip down to Lake Laberge proved a respite from frequent alarms, though sodden weather kept us in a continual state of chill dampness. When the clouds lifted, however, we were treated to constant daylight, the summer solstice being almost upon us.

When the sun broke through at brief intervals, the Yukon was a rich emerald colour of great beauty. The high cut banks showed evidence of the constant erosion of their sandy faces. The current, at times, assumed a more leisurely pace, encouraging lassitude during the long afternoons. Wood camps, devouring the trees for riverboat cordwood and other signs of human habitation, appeared at times. Sternwheelers, with their insatiable appetite for fuel, now plied the river, replacing many of the smaller and more primitive craft.

Evening encampment was a welcome respite from the long hours aboard the cutter. But there, we faced another misery. The mosquitoes were ravenous, and after the long days of rain, massive clouds of the creatures plagued our every move. Holmes puffed energetically on his pipe, emitting great clouds of smoke, but even this offered little respite.

"Yukon mosquitoes are said to be able to carry off young eagles," Corporal Pipes offered cheerfully.

"I can well imagine," said I. "The sooner we move on, the better. These beasts will leave us anaemic if we linger too long."

Lake Laberge showed varied signs of the human tide that had flowed over and around its waters in the last two years. As at so many points from Skagway, the detritus of civilization stood as rude intrusion in the wilderness landscape—pitiful shacks, abandoned cargo, emptied containers of every sort; at water's edge, flimsy piers, half-submerged craft. Remarkably, I found a wooden case filled with tins of Oxo. Happily, I appropriated several of them to supplement our diminished supplies. Did not these bouillon cubes sustain the builders of empire on many a frontier?

"Corporal, tell me, do you happen to know the enterprising young fellow with the stream launch?" Holmes asked as he pointed to a sizable craft that lay idly, moored some fifty yards from where we had made camp.

"I do. Fine chap. Dependable and hard-working. McDonald's his name. He's done well for himself without bothering to rush on to the gold fields," Pipes replied.

"I thought as much. I judge him a man of character and integrity. Would you say he is a patriot?" Holmes continued.

"True blue. A good man and loyal. A loyal Canadian." "Loyal. Ah, that's the key. I have observed him since our arrival, and I think he can be of service to his country. If you will be good enough to introduce us, I would like a word with him."

As always, Holmes's keen powers of observation seemed to have provided him with the person he needed, for what purpose I could not guess. We surely did not need additional transportation. Pipes was proving admirably capable at that point.

"While Corporal Pipes and I have a word with Mr McDonald, perhaps you and Devlin can prepare for our departure." With that Holmes strode off with the Corporal, leaving me—and I suspect Devlin, too—curious about his designs. As always, I knew Holmes would clarify matters in his own time. We proceeded to break camp. By the time the two returned, Devlin and I had stored the gear, and the campsite was clear. Holmes wore a slight smile and seemed well satisfied with his visit to young McDonald. The Corporal appeared slightly bewildered.

I will not burden the reader with a detailed account of our continuing voyage downriver. The wilderness seemed endless, signs of human habitation scarce. We passed bleak Indian villages occasionally, finding it best to keep our visits to them short. The Five Finger Rapids provided some moments of great anxiety. Five great reddish rocks loomed ahead, seeming intent upon our destruction. Our pilot, however, boldly chose an opening that proved to be about a hundred feet wide, swept forward, and after a drop of perhaps two feet, shot through a vicious return curl, taking in not more than a bucket or two of water. Scarcely six miles further, my concern was renewed by the ominous roar of the Rink Rapids that mercifully proved to be more sound than fury. Pipes, by keeping to the right, took us through in almost smooth waters. Knowledge of the peculiarities of the river paid handsomely.

Fort Selkirk, the site of a Hudson's Bay Company post for half a century, still boasting a few buildings belonging now to the Alaska Commercial Company, provided brief relief from the monotony of forest and stream. Athabaskans and their ever-present dogs greeted us from the high and slippery embankment. We did not dally long, despite the fact that this was as much of a community as we had seen in a very long time.

The days passed uneventfully, often blending into each other. I welcomed Corporal Pipes's announcement, therefore, as we made camp under the hazy late afternoon sunlight.

"We should make Stewart City in a day or so, and then it's but eighty miles to Dawson," Pipes asserted with a stab at encouragement, given the miseries of the perpetual plague of bloodsucking creatures.

"That is grand," said Devlin. "We should be there by the fourth of July then."

"Oh yes, the worst is behind us. We'll make it in time for Dominion Day, if I don't miss my guess," Pipes answered.

Holmes looked thoughtfully at the Mounted Policeman and then at our Gaelic companion of so many miles. Clearly, his splendid mind was occupied with weighty matters and grave thoughts.

"Dominion Day. Yes, that would be appropriate," said Holmes. "The British North America Act. The Dominion of Canada. An interesting experiment in a thoroughly contradictory concept—divided sovereignty. But it seems to work. At least it is vastly superior to the American brand of independence."

"Indeed it is," said I. "It is a glorious thought to contemplate this magnificent and untamed land as yet another segment of the British Empire."

Corporal Pipes smiled broadly. "We Canadians are proud to be British, but we're also proud to be Canadian," he asserted in his flat Canadian accent.

"Bloody monsters," growled Devlin, slapping a satiated mosquito on his cheek.

Stewart City, while it represented the only sign of a human community we had seen in some time, did not offer much in the way of civilized amenities. For an extortive price, we were able to obtain hot baths, which did something to soothe the aching muscles and joints, though little to relieve the annoyance of the countless insect bites that covered us from head to toe. Nonetheless, a day's layover there did something to lift my spirits. Our journey was almost at an end.

As I stood contemplating the expanse of the river, which now ran a light brown, not the rich emerald of the upper reaches of the Yukon, Holmes joined me. The hour was late, but the perpetual daylight seemed to rob one of the normal sense of time.

"You've been a brick," said Holmes. "This venture has not been easy on men of our years, and yet we have not only survived, but, by the look of you, flourished."

"It's good of you to say so, though I must confess I feel my years," I replied.

"And now the finale is at hand. I have a feeling that we will arrive in Dawson none too soon."

"The Puget Sound Cavalry?" I asked, still uncertain as to whether Holmes had chosen the right course with them, making no attempt to prevent their continued progress.

"Oh, they are no longer a factor to be reckoned with. Mr McDonald's sturdy little vessel has by now delivered a barge loaded with men and horses to the far shores of Lake Laberge, where the Maxim guns of the Yukon Field Force should be persuading our filibusterers to lay down their arms and accept temporary detainment as a small price for the rashness of their deeds."

"The Yukon Field Force?" I asked.

"Yes. Conveniently just arrived overland from Edmonton and ready to defend the interests of the Dominion. McDonald took no persuading to expedite the transit of the APSC. With the largest and most seaworthy barge on the lake, the cavalry company could easily be convinced that the deal he offered them could be matched neither in price nor efficiency. Then it will be only a matter of delivering them to the Canadian military, regarding whose whereabouts Corporal Pipes had recently been informed."

"I must say, I am relieved. You are certain that McDonald will be successful?"

"If I am any judge of quality and character, I am convinced that the young man will carry off the caper with panache and turn a personal profit at the same time," Holmes chuckled. "Patriotism and profit: what could be a more rewarding prospect!"

"The Yukon is certainly safer," I said.

"Threats to law and order come in varying guises. I am sure you have not forgotten that the chief mischief maker–'the Piper'–continues to elude us. And who knows how many Fenians and other malcontents are still planning other forms of trouble?"

We lapsed into silence. The great orb of the sun brushed the horizon. Aside from the ever-present mosquitoes, the scene was bucolic. I drew my pocket watch and was surprised to see that it was five minutes to midnight. What a truly remarkable land!

DAWSON

It was mid-afternoon, with the temperature pushing, unbelievably, into the nineties (Fahrenheit), when we caught our first glimpse of our destination—or so we thought.

"No, no. That, gentlemen, is Klondike City, vulgarly known as Lousetown. A place of the lowest reputation. The dregs, the absolute dregs. What vice and human folly, I would not venture to guess," Pipes intoned. "Dawson lies on the farther bank of that stream—the Klondike."

To the north of the river that entered the Yukon on our right, we saw an assortment of structures that looked little more promising than the hovels abreast of us. Several rows of rough wooden structures lay in the flats beyond the embankment, joined by a straggling assortment of tents clinging to the hillside, shabby white rectangles against the dark green of the forested slopes. Humped above them was a sizeable mountain gashed by a gigantic yellow-grey slide.

"That," announced Pipes, our still cheerful guide, "is known as 'the Moosehide.'"

Full attention had to be given to guiding our craft across to the right bank beyond the point where the sparkling clear waters of the Klondike emptied into the Yukon. The surging silt-laden current of the latter fought to carry us on downstream, but Pipes skilfully brought us to the shore among a profusion of crafts and shacks such as I had never seen before or since.

"Dawson, gentlemen—the golden city," the corporal announced with a jesting bow.

"A city? It looks more like a bog about to swallow every plank and post laid down by man," exclaimed Devlin.

"An Irishman should feel right at home then," Holmes observed with a disarming smile. "No offense intended, Mr Devlin."

We stepped ashore to survey the metropolis of the north. Its very existence in the vast primordial landscape seemed totally incongruous. An amazing riot of saw board structures, whose variety was almost infinite, stood in roughly parallel rows along the cluttered thoroughfares that passed for streets. Cordwood, discarded crates, mud, and dung stood everywhere. Dogs and horses seemed in abundant supply. Remarkably, electrical power poles stood at intervals, and their wires festooned the streets, competing for space with a most remarkable assortment of signs announcing business enterprises of almost limitless variety. *How, I asked myself, could such a place spring from utter wilderness in but three short years?*

As in Skagway, the saloons were clearly the most popular establishments, regardless of the time of day or night. Few people were on the streets as we moved up from the river.

"My word!" I exclaimed, realizing that tomorrow was the first of July–Dominion Day. "Why is there not more sign of celebration? Is not this the eve of the great Canadian holiday?"

"It is, indeed," said Pipes, "and there will be celebrating enough among us Canadians, but the sad truth of the matter is that 90 per cent of the population is American."

"An American city under British jurisdiction," mused Devlin.

"And a perfect setting for mischief," said I. I was only partly reassured by the numerous Union Jacks that flew here and there among canvas banners beckoning the gold seeker to everything from the Odd Fellows to the grand opening of Godfrey's Laundry, where mending was done free with a wash.

Our introduction to Dawson was only nicely begun when Corporal Pipes, our worthy guide, suddenly snapped to attention. Approaching us was a figure of undoubted importance. His scarlet tunic immaculate, with its polished buttons reflecting in the brilliance of the late afternoon sun, he strode towards us with the firm assurance of one accustomed to authority. His ample handlebar moustache was trimmed and waxed to perfection. One sensed greatness.

"Samuel B. Steele, Superintendent of the Northwest Mounted Police in the Yukon," he announced in a stentorian voice.

It was clear that Steele had been briefed on our progress. And it was equally clear that the Superintendent saw no need for any assistance in managing the peace and order of the Klondike populace, law abiding or lawless. Nonetheless, he treated us with courtesy and even consideration.

While Corporal Pipes and Devlin saw to the transfer of our baggage from the cutter to our hotel, Steele graciously invited Holmes and me to a rather joyless office in a plain log structure. Offering us mugs of coffee from an enamel pot upon the small wood stove, the Superintendent explained to us that NWMP headquarters lay on a sizable piece of land to the south of the town site.

"Our presence in the territory is well established. The detachment is sufficient in number and more than sufficient in competence," Steele asserted. The brief silence that followed this statement seemed designed to give us pause for thought.

"For reasons that are understandable, both Ottawa and London have deemed it wise to keep your identities secret, but for one who is used to the ways of politicians and officialdom, it takes little imagination to arrive at your true identities." He paused with a hint of a smile escaping from below his ample moustache.

"It is evident to me who you are. And I welcome you to this wilderness Eldorado."

Steele paused dramatically, his scarlet tunic again catching my attention and calling to mind the proud British traditions of global mission.

"You are, of course, the famous Sherlock Holmes, together with your Boswell, Dr Watson."

So there it was! Our elaborate and somewhat silly masquerade had come to naught.

Holmes smiled broadly. "I had long since concluded that this attempt at subterfuge might pass muster with simple minds but would stand no chance with any man of perceptivity. And I had no intention of even attempting this charade with you."

(I wondered if this were true, given the rigor of my friend's insistence on the pseudonyms during the early days of our journey.)

As the Superintendent recounted for us the remarkable history and amazing statistics of his community, we were properly impressed with the problems his jurisdiction presented.

Dawson was nothing less than a man-made miracle, wrestled out of the most uninviting piece of real estate that one could imagine. For many months, the berg was bound in the numbing fetters of sub-zero cold and perpetual darkness. Escaping this, it often suffered alternating bouts of flood or heat wave. The cross section of human habitation seemed to mirror the extremes of nature.

It was said that Dawson rivalled Seattle in size, and amazingly, it seemed to me much larger—though far more haphazard—than Vancouver. One would hardly describe it as a city. It was more like a giant bazaar, with humanity of every description busily pursuing a thousand unseen purposes. Steele contended that, for every dream fulfilled, there were scores of bitter disappointments. A community that survived so perilously close to the brink of catastrophe produced the best and noblest, as well as the worst and basest. Man-made disasters clearly rivalled nature's. Charred remains of a massive fire some two months ago were evident everywhere, but the rebuilding process was well under way.

The hotel, to which Superintendent Steele guided us as he briefed us on his community, was itself in the process of reconstruction. The structure was of a markedly less primitive design architecturally than its predecessor, lost recently to the flames.

Arriving at the lobby entrance, Steele suggested that we get some rest and strode off imperiously down the elevated boardwalk, nodding to the many who tipped their hats or otherwise showed their respect for him. It was apparent that Samuel Steele was very much in charge of the affairs of this fledgling metropolis. It was said that Steele was not beyond the arbitrary banishment of those he saw as incorrigible. If this smacked of despotism, it was at least a benevolent variety. And order prevailed where so clearly the elements of chaos existed.

It was equally clear that, although he was correct in his relations with us, he had no sense of needing our assistance in handling any eventuality that might arise.

Our room, which overlooked the very noisy street below, had clearly just been completed. The pleasures of even simple comforts had almost been forgotten, and I looked longingly towards the bed. As if reading my thoughts, Holmes reminded me that time was short and that the whole reason for our journey now demanded our greatest effort.

"Think, Watson, think! Put yourself in the position of one who would wish to wrest this land from the Crown." Holmes clearly did not intend to spend time in bed. For long minutes, he stared intently out the window at the street below, deeply engrossed in his thoughts. At length, I joined him, interrupting his reverie.

"It seems little short of outrageous that so many Yankee flags should festoon the streets of this outpost of the Empire," I observed indignantly, leaning out the window to see the Stars and Stripes that fluttered from innumerable poles down the length of the street. "In a place where only the Union Jack and the Red Ensign should fly, why is such a practice permitted?"

"Our Superintendent Steele is no fool. He knows he walks a very narrow line between order and anarchy. To permit what may be safely overlooked and focus one's energies on what he cannot afford to overlook is the mark of a leader," Holmes responded. "Better a few symbolic gestures to American hubris than a showdown that might exhaust the meagre resources at his disposal."

"But surely, with tomorrow being Dominion Day—" I protested.

"With the vast majority of the residents of this nascent metropolis citizens of the United States of America, it will take both tact and determination to preserve Her Gracious Majesty's authority here."

"Is Steele up to it?" I asked anxiously.

"He has done a fine job of it, I am sure, but he shall have our help whether he requests it or not. There cannot be too many minds addressing the problem."

Looking at the varied segments of mankind that dodged and wound their ways along the crowded wooden walks or skirted the ubiquitous mud puddles and challenged the assorted carts and cursing drovers who vied for position in the rutted maze called Second Street, I could feel nothing but admiration for anyone who had been able to prevent this wilderness community from descending into a state reminiscent of bedlam.

Even as we viewed the scene below, a large wagon, pulled by two lumbering draught horses, collided with a cart drawn by a shabby brown mare. The cart tipped, dropping its driver and several wooden barrels into the dirt and forcing the pathetic animal to its knees. The shrill neigh of the beast and the explosive vulgarities of the driver produced an immediate knot of babbling contentious bystanders.

Shaking his head, Holmes turned from the window and seemed again lost in reverie. As if speaking only to himself, he muttered, "Tomorrow is Dominion Day, but the Fourth of July is the occasion when Sam Steele will have his mettle tested. Whose writ will run in the Klondike?"

In the street, Corporal Pipes appeared and, with gentle persuasion, stemmed the ripening crisis. Such was the reputation of the Force—and from what I witnessed, justly deserved. Still, Holmes looked concerned.

During this lengthy journey, I had tasted a great variety of fare in a great variety of eating establishments, but I can tell the reader that, when Holmes and I ventured into the Monte Carlo that evening, the atmosphere surpassed anything I had ever imagined possible in the civilized world. The din was beyond that of a thousand Billingsgate fishwives or even the roar of the rapids at Whitehorse. The food, though expensive, was scarcely identifiable by sight or by smell. Most objectionable, I suppose, was the fact that the principal source of the tumult was clearly a very loud and boisterous hoard of Americans.

"It is clear that we made a bad choice in trying to eat here," said Holmes, as a burly imbiber bumped him, causing him to spill the last of his coffee—or what passed for coffee. "But one can learn a good deal simply by observing the mood and inclinations of a mob of this sort."

It was difficult to hear him amid the pandemonium. "Well, if it were the Yanks you wanted to assess, there clearly would be few better places than this," I replied.

At that moment, a giant of a fellow climbed atop the bar and bellowed like the Land's End foghorn for silence. Remarkably, the establishment fell relatively quiet.

"Now hear me," he demanded, brandishing a large whiskey bottle in a ham-like fist. "As July approaches, it seems to me that all red-blooded Americans, separated from homeland and family, must think of appropriate means to celebrate the birth of our glorious republic. Ain't that right, Black Prince?" He turned to a muscular Negro who stood near the bar, dressed in a light grey linen suit, which seemed singularly out of place in this northern clime.

"It is. It surely is," the black man nodded.

"And we intend to have a celebration this place will never forget," continued the speaker atop the bar. "We'll have a parade to beat all parades. Fireworks. A great prize fight, with Black Prince here taking on all comers. Ain't that right!"

Throughout the crowd there were grunts of approval, and some lusty cheers. If there were any Canadians in the room or any English other than ourselves, they did not make their presence known—wisely, I suspect. Holmes leaned back in his chair, a bemused smile on his face.

"We certainly came to the right place," he declared over the din.

"I nominate Captain Jack for parade marshal," called someone from the far side of the room.

"Seconded," another voice followed.

"Great idea," the hulk on the bar boomed. "Captain Jack Crawford—Civil War hero, Indian fighter, and … and illustrious resident of our fair town is nominated! All in favour, say aye."

A rising wave of approval swept the room.

"It's done then. And that ain't all. Our own Consul, none other than the official representative of the good old US of A will be here to … to show the flag, so to speak." He chortled heartily.

But at the mention of the Consul, I noted that Holmes's eyes narrowed and alarm passed like a fleeting shadow over his angular features.

"It is time we were going," he said, nodding towards the door. We rose as quickly as the press of bodies in the place would permit, and we threaded our way to the doorway and made our exit as the crowd resumed its noisy revelry.

The Arctic sky was still light, despite the late hour. As we strode along the rough planking of the walk, Holmes outlined his latest assessment of the impending crisis.

"Given that serious military adventurism is unlikely at the present—and given the ineffectiveness of the cavalry unit, which I suspect, even now, is guest of the Yukon Field Force—we are back to our original concern: terrorism and Patrick the Piper."

"He has scarcely been out of my thoughts, but I confess, I am as much at a loss as ever to know how we shall ever identify him. There are enough Irishmen here to fill every gaol in London, Dublin, and Glasgow."

"I fear you do not exaggerate," Holmes agreed.

"And what diabolical scheme will he hatch?" I asked in despair.

"Take heart, my good man. Fortunately, most of these Hibernians are only interested in gold and care nothing for political causes of any kind. As to the Piper's diabolical scheme—as you so aptly put it—we need to focus our reasoning powers as sharply as we can."

"Terrorists have proven very inventive," I said.

"You are right, certainly. The terrorist finds the way to extract the maximum effect from his act. Since he cannot dictate circumstances, his inventiveness consists in selecting a way of using them to his own purposes."

"Utterly without conscience," I asserted.

"Not conscience as you and I perceive it," Holmes continued. "The point to remember, however, is that he acts not because of the strength but the weakness of his position. Were he strong enough, he would alter affairs by edict or decree. If Patrick the Piper were strong enough, he would will the British off the face of the earth. But he cannot, so he resorts to unpredictable and outrageous acts of violence in the hope that eventually circumstances will be changed."

"And how can we anticipate anything he is likely to do?"

"Let us look carefully at the present circumstances," Holmes continued. "We have a large, even overwhelming, population of Americans here on Canadian soil. We have a long history of American expansionism, often turned in a northerly direction. And when will patriotic fervour reach its peak?" He paused for my response.

"Why, the Fourth of July, of course."

"So the time seems almost assured, does it not?"

"You are right. It is perfectly logical," I concurred.

"And what is it we know about the modus operandi of this shadowy figure we've been seeking since our afternoon at the Travellers?"

"Well, he's a cold-blooded killer, an assassin without conscience or human sensibilities."

"Exactly! And where is one most likely to find a victim who will stir the greatest outrage among these—"

Holmes broke off in mid-sentence, for we had reached the entrance of our hotel, and several guests were stepping out onto the boardwalk, laughing raucously. I must say, one or two of the female members of the party appeared to be women of easy virtue. Such were far from uncommon in this boisterous community.

By the time we had reached our room, the chilling outlines of what Holmes seemed to be inferring began to dawn on me. I recalled the look on Holmes's face at the mention of the American Consul.

"Surely," I gasped to him as we closed the door, "you do not think the Consul might be the target?"

"Not an unreasonable conclusion," Holmes replied. "Why, if he were killed, it would be a colossal embarrassment to civil authority in the entire territory," I continued.

"It would confirm the assertion that the Canadians are incapable of preserving order—a claim the Yanks never tire of making," Holmes added. "One need only peruse the *Klondike Nugget* to see the charges of Canadian government ineptness as a constant theme. The paper is clearly the local voice of American chauvinism."

"And once the wrath of the American populace was ignited, the task of maintaining law and order might be more than Steele and all of his men could ever hope to achieve," I said.

"You are getting the picture," Holmes replied.

"Yes, by Jove, I can see how such action would challenge the stability of society itself," said I with mounting agitation. "It could result in destabilization—"

"Watson, Watson, the threat to civil order is bad enough. Do not imperil the Queen's English as well. May we never live to see the day a verbal atrocity such as *destabilization* will enter the language." Holmes laughed heartily.

At that moment, a loud explosion sounded nearby. We rushed to the window, Holmes throwing aside the coarsely woven curtain. With relief, we saw that an exuberant group of Canadians—I assumed they were Canadians—had ignited a pyrotechnic device. Dominion Day celebrations were apparently already in progress. Glancing at my watch, I noted that it was one minute past midnight, July 1. One found it difficult to get used to these Yukon summer nights.

Dominion Day festivities were fervent but not particularly exuberant. One could plainly see that this metropolis of the north was not really a Canadian town in many respects. Since fewer than one in five residents was Canadian, the indifference of the alien population appeared to dilute the celebrations. The magisterial Samuel Steele made a very acceptable speech to a sizeable crowd of patriots who assembled at noon before the newly rebuilt city hall. Picnics, foot races, and a bedraggled parade of local dignitaries led by a handful of Mounted Police without mounts provided diversion for the citizens who could rejoice in the fact that they were fortunate enough to be subjects of Her Imperial Majesty on this arctic frontier. Two pipers pierced the air with the wail of their barbaric instruments, reminding me painfully of this ubiquitous tradition of the British presence worldwide. More chilling, however, was the reminder that the object of our long journey—that diabolic Irish piper—had continued to confound our efforts.

"Steele is clearly a man of courage and ability," said Holmes as we returned to our rooms after viewing the festivities.

"Indeed he is," I agreed.

"And he has done a commendable job of taming this fledgling community. These Yanks, to whom sidearms are so natural, must either surrender them or acquire a license. And I gather that licenses are hard to come by."

"Commendable, commendable," I concurred.

"I shall be very busy for the next two days. I hope to delve more deeply into the alien element of this community, and I shall have to resort to disguise to do so. Watson, I want you and Devlin to assist me."

"Of course, Holmes, whatever you need."

"Devlin can penetrate the Hiberian lairs for us. Have him report to you anything that might suggest a plot or a conspiracy arising from that source."

"I will. He's a sharp-witted fellow."

"And you. I want you to provide a liaison with Colonel Steele. He is, of course, not enamoured with our presence here, but as a servant of Her Majesty's Government, he will accept our assistance as he has been ordered to do. We must make it as palatable for him as we can. And if that means showing deference to his prestige and authority, we can surely do that."

"I will be a model of diplomacy and deference," I chuckled.

"I'm sure you will. Restrained flattery goes a long way with the brightest of these colonials," Holmes smiled. "No one is able to convey sincerity more adequately than you, my Boswell."

Soon Holmes was fast asleep, and I sat for some time looking out the window towards the grey hump of rock that rose beyond the wild array of buildings that comprised this city in the wilderness. When at last I lay down, sleep came quickly, and when I awoke in the morning,

Holmes was gone. After dressing hurriedly, I crossed the hall to knock on Devlin's door. With his seemingly inexhaustible supply of good spirits, he invited me in and listened carefully as I outlined the duties Holmes had assigned him.

As it turned out, I did not have to seek out Steele. As Devlin and I stepped into the street from our hotel, his resonant voice greeted us.

"Ah, gentlemen, as luck would have it, I have decided to enlist the help of our newly arrived experts in criminal investigation in a modest project."

"Well, sir, we are at your command," I responded, ignoring the note of sarcasm I seemed to detect.

"Where is your compatriot?" he asked, looking beyond Devlin and myself to the dusky interior of the lobby.

"Unfortunately, he left very early this morning, and I am at a loss to say exactly where he is," I confessed. "But I am sure we can assist you."

Steele took me by the arm and guided me down the walk away from any doors and windows. With an air of confidentiality, he glanced up and down the street before he began to speak to us.

"Confidential sources, which I am not at liberty to reveal, inform me that a major civil disturbance has been planned by certain alien elements who have been trying to capitalize on the discontent and natural disregard for law and order that characterized a large segment of our residents."

"I am not surprised," I interjected, thinking of our many conversations on this very subject.

"I have tried to walk a thin line between allowing the more unruly element to vent its pent-up energies and the necessity of upholding cherished Canadian traditions with respect to everything from Sabbath observance to liquor and gambling."

"Commendable, commendable," I mumbled, though frankly I found Canadian practices unusually exacting and even puritanical.

"I've given many a rowdy a blue ticket to leave town, but many more have been suffered to pursue their common habits, so long as they avoided outright cheating, obscenity, or moral outrage. Unfortunately, not everyone in public employ has been as scrupulous as one might desire, and cases of graft and corruption are sadly not lacking. Overall, however, I think we have maintained a civilized level of government, of law and order."

Steele paused somewhat dramatically. His magnificent handlebar moustache glistened with droplets of perspiration. It was amazing how positively hot a day could be this close to the Arctic Circle.

"But, gentlemen, I apologize, perhaps if you will join me in my office, I can explain to you what role you may play in rescuing this great territory from the grasp of greedy adventurers."

"At your convenience," I said.

"Good. Shall we say eleven this morning. And it would be ideal if your associate could join us."

"I'm not sure that is possible, but I will try to locate him."

Steele turned away to be soon accosted by a number of citizens who, as I had previously noted, obviously seemed to regard him as the incarnation of law and order. With a commanding beneficence, he listened to their concerns as he made his regal progress towards the office of the NWMP.

"Well, this is a turn of affairs," said Devlin.

"Indeed it is," I agreed. "I wonder why suddenly he has found it useful to seek our assistance when he has previously left the impression that he believed he needed none."

"Being Irish makes me suspicious, you know," said Devlin.

"Oh, and what are you suspicious of right now?"

"I believe perhaps the good colonel is not so anxious for our help as he is to put us where he can know what we're up to."

"Ridiculous. A gentleman recognizes a gentleman when he sees one. Quality will always prevail."

"A gentleman you may be, but yours truly is not so fortunate," Devlin responded.

"Devlin, my good man, I should think that the mere fact that you have accompanied Housman—Holmes—and myself should speak for your qualities as a gentleman."

I was taken aback by this sudden display of humility, though I reckoned that no Irishman could ever really pass for a gentleman, even in this primitive setting.

At eleven o'clock promptly, Devlin and I arrived at the quarters of the NWMP. Steele welcomed us without fanfare and showed us into his spartan office. Clearly, he was a man who stood on little ceremony.

"I see your colleague, Holmes, is not with you," he observed in an accusatory tone.

"Unfortunately, I have no idea where he has gone. But I am certain that, wherever he is, he is attending to the matter at hand," I assured him.

"Well that may be. I intend no slight to you, but I confess that your friend's reputation is the one thing that keeps me from demanding that Ottawa leave things to me."

"We intend nothing but to be as helpful as we are able, I assure you," I rejoined.

"I am sure that is true, and because I am a firm believer in the unity of the Empire, I have found a way in which you can be helpful—at least Devlin—"

I felt a mild sense of rebuff and distress at this slight to my person.

"If you were to circulate naturally among the hotheads whom my sources tell me meet nightly at O'Leary's plotting mischief for everything British and drinking to the ill-health of the Queen, it may be you can pick up some intelligence nuggets that will help lead us to a strike in the mother lode."

"It's as good as done," Devlin smiled.

With that, Devlin was gone, and I stood alone in the chilly presence of Steele. It unnerved me a bit to feel so inferior to one who, after all, was only a colonial. But the man was properly polite, and it was clear that his dedication to Her Majesty was genuine.

"We have but two days to complete our investigations and put our plans in place. And in case you have any doubts about the thoroughness of my work, I will outline my preparations," Steele stated, somewhat loftily.

There followed from him in the next few minutes an outline of precautionary measures and planned options to meet any conceivable eventualities. I must confess, however, that this recitation seemed to me perfunctory and only a formal fulfilling of his duty to be cooperative with Her Majesty's representative than from any notion that anyone other than himself could meet the anticipated challenges. With the deference of a callow subaltern, I listened, nodding approvingly, though I chaffed inwardly at the patronizing tone I detected.

"And so you see, sir, that preparations are as adequate as humanly possible. Neither Ottawa nor London could possibly improve on them. I trust you will convey that fact to Whitehall or Downing Street or to whomever you report."

"Of course we will. You may be assured," I replied.

No sooner were the words out of my mouth than my mind focused on the horrible image of failure and the implications for Holmes and myself, who had come these thousands of miles because of the confidence Her Majesty's Government had had in us. Failure would surely sully Holmes's reputation. A lifetime of dedication to service would be negated. Such thoughts, however, were entirely selfish and unworthy. Far more important was the peril to Empire that the near future held. I felt ashamed as I took my leave of the commander of the Yukon.

The next two days seemed interminable. Devlin having gone to circulate among his countrymen and other such elements as might prove the source of trouble, I wandered and worried alone. Holmes did not return to our hotel, and I heard not a word from him. I trusted that his absence was still intentional and that no harm had befallen him. My own capacity to assist in meeting whatever mischief was afoot for law and order in the territory seemed slight. My role as liaison with Steele seemed empty. But I determined to make myself useful by being as vigilant as possible, and accordingly, I spent considerable time in close observation of the activities of Main Street, where the preparations for the American Independence Day parade were proceeding noisily, if not particularly efficiently. I must confess the prospect of doing anything significant towards the preservation of good government and civility seemed remote. The relatively small force of Mounties charged with preserving the peace seemed pathetically inadequate in terms of the unruly hordes that had made this place their home in recent months.

FOURTH OF JULY

The fourth of July morning was cloudless and mild. Given the long arctic days and the uninterrupted chain of light, riotous revelry and all the varieties of celebration the human species had devised proceeded unabated around the clock.

At noon, the gala parade began its triumphal, if somewhat chaotic, procession down the street, the red, white, and blue bunting spanning sharply in the breeze. Most unsettling was the riot of American flags that festooned the false-front buildings that constituted the hotel and business district of the Babel of the north. The rain having stopped, the streets were by now showing signs of transforming themselves from a quagmire into a fine powdered grey dust.

Triumphant upon a great roan came Captain Jack Crawford, grand marshal of the parade. His swagger and confidence were typically American. Close by him and with an equal degree of bravado and self-importance rode the American Consul, McCook, whose ample girth cascaded over his belt in grand corpulence, threatening to spill out beyond the cantle of his saddle.

Despite the festive atmosphere, I felt a great sense of foreboding. Perhaps it was because these Yanks seemed to have no sense that this was the sovereign territory of Her Imperial Majesty. More particularly, it was because, after our lengthy journey, the moment of truth had arrived, and we seemed so inadequately prepared to meet it. It was in the midst of these very reveries that I suddenly caught sight of some unusual commotion, which began to unfold before my eyes with a nightmarish deliberateness. I shall never forget the agonizing seconds, which, at the time, seemed to stretch into unbearable minutes.

As McCook smiled and waved expansively to the throng of spectators crowding the parade's path, our colleague of these many miles, Devlin, stepped forth from among a noisy group of miners, whose brogue gave away their Irish lineage. With amazing deliberation and a coolness that defied normal behaviour, he drew a pistol from his jacket and raised it towards the Consul, whose great bulk towered above the rabble—a target that could scarcely be missed.

"He's got a gun!" someone shouted.

As if by reflex, a red-coated figure leaped from the elevated wooden walk opposite my own position.

"No, no," a woman's voice cried.

It was clear that the Mountie was too far from the Consul to prevent the imminent tragedy.

In that instant, I launched myself into the street, desperate to prevent the inevitable. But before I had taken two steps, I saw—again the timeless absurdity that catastrophic events often acquire in retrospect—a second Irishman who stood near Devlin reach out with lightning speed and deliver a smashing blow to his extended arm. The flash and the jolting crack punctuated the scene in a heart-stopping climax. Smoke and dust filled the air. Horses rearing, men diving for cover, women swooning—all of these impressions imprinted themselves forever on my retinas. I felt a searing pain in my leg as I reeled backwards to come to rest upon my posterior on the edge of the wooden sidewalk from which I had just leaped.

"He's shot. He's killed," someone yelled.

"Only wounded. He's okay," came another voice.

"Who's dead?" I demanded, envisioning the Consul mortally wounded—mortally wounded by our friend and associate Cromwell Devlin! My mind strained at the incongruity of it all.

"He's all right. See, it's only his leg."

As my vision cleared, I realized that it was I who occupied the attention of this segment of the crowd.

"Zounds, man. What of the Consul?" I demanded in an agony of suspense.

"Fine. Untouched, in fact." The scarlet-clad Corporal leaned reassuringly over me.

Elbowing through the crowd to kneel next to the young Mountie was the Irishman whose split-second action had deflected Devlin's aim. His craggy features were indelibly etched in my brain.

"How? What?" I stammered, struggling to make sense of these fantastic and incongruous images that savaged my brain.

"I believe you've taken, in your leg, the bullet intended for the Consul," the fellow observed, gently pulling at my pant leg, which I now say was turning a dark red with my blood.

"Terribly sorry about this. I should have diverted the shot upward."

My senses sharpening as I looked towards the speaker, I realized with mixed chagrin and amusement that this Hibernian ruffian was none other than Holmes himself, in yet another of his endless array of baffling disguises.

The dawning light of recognition in my eyes drew from him a broad grin and a mischievous wink. "Doctor, I fear you shall have to have this wound attended to promptly."

"That I will, Holmes," I rejoined.

And with that, I apparently lost consciousness.

The smell of disinfectant and the feel of soft linens assailed my senses. Holmes's angular features registered as the mists lifted from me.

"Feeling better, doctor?" The voice too was Holmes's—comfortably familiar.

As full consciousness returned, I recognized the modest appointments of our hotel room.

"Only a flesh wound," said Holmes. "You will be up and about in a day or two—in time for us to begin the long journey home."

"But another wound to add to my collection," I murmured, remembering that distant day on the far-off Indian subcontinent.

"Her Majesty's Government will be grateful," Holmes smiled.

"But alas, how ignominious. To blunder into the path of a stray bullet. All this way and my feeble efforts were useless.

In truth, Holmes, I was nothing but a useless spectator. A useless—"

"Enough of that, my dear Watson. You were magnificent. Without you, this entire devilish plot would likely have succeeded."

"Holmes, Holmes. Don't patronize me. I know you mean well but—"

"I do not engage in idle flattery. You have known me long enough to know that. Nor would I insult an old friend by patronizing him."

At that moment, a knock sounded at the door.

"Come in," said Holmes, turning from the bed.

In the doorway stood the magnificent figure of Samuel Benfield Steele.

"Good afternoon, gentlemen," he said warmly. He shook Holmes's hand in a clear gesture of appreciation. Then he strode to the bed where I lay. "I shall never be able to thank you enough, gentlemen, for your services to the Yukon—and to myself."

He grasped my hand in his ham-like grip and smiled so broadly that his luxuriant moustache curled into a great glistening *U*.

"But," I stammered, "I did nothing. At the very moment of crisis, I did nothing."

"And that was precisely what was needed at the crucial juncture. So confident was the enemy that you and your colleague, Holmes—or Housman, if you like—would have a closely coordinated scheme that your indecisiveness and desultory actions of the last twenty-four hours utterly baffled them. They sought to make sense out of actions that had no particular rationale to them and thus sought subtle and significant meaning in your behaviour that was, of course, not there."

"Absolutely, Watson," Holmes injected. "The enemy had reason to believe that any action taken by us would be taken jointly. So when the showdown came, he—they—"

"But how was he—were they—so well aware of our—" I raised myself to a half-sitting position in the bed, the pain in my leg forgotten for the moment.

The smile that crossed Holmes's face had a rare quality of triumph in it. He looked at Steele with obvious satisfaction. The world's greatest consulting detective and this heroic figure of the northland clearly shared the deepest respect for each other.

"They also serve who only stand and wait," the Colonel said generously.

It may be that Holmes and Steele were seeking to be kind and to assuage my embarrassment, but I can assure the reader that their efforts to buoy my spirits were entirely successful. Two more noble spirits would be hard to find.

"But you need your rest," Steele continued, backing towards the door.

By now, my mind was clearing, and the confused images that had assailed me during the attack on Consul McCook returned with a vengeance.

"But wait," I cried. "Did my eyes deceive me? I thought for a moment I saw Devlin.... It was Devlin I saw raising the.... It was you, Holmes, who so quickly deflected the shot. Of course, I didn't realize at the time, but—"

"Wait a minute, my good man," Holmes said, raising a hand of protest. "Wait a minute. I'm sure we can put your mind at ease. But rest is the most important thing for you right now. Remember, neither of us is as young as we used to be."

"It will take some explaining, but I am sure two such firm friends will enjoy the task together. And duty yet calls me. I will say goodbye for now. If I can assist you in any way, let me know. We are grateful." With that, the Colonel left, his heavy footfalls diminishing down the bare wooden planking of the hotel corridor.

I lay back, conscious of my exhaustion. Holmes must have soon fallen asleep also.

When I awoke, Holmes was pouring water from the great china pitcher into the basin, his razor strop on his shoulder. Bright sunlight flooded the room. He turned as I stirred.

"Feeling better?" he asked.

My leg throbbed, but I was happy to respond cheerfully.

As Holmes lathered his angular face, my mind returned to the many unanswered questions that still bedevilled me.

"Tell me, Holmes, was that Devlin, or does he have a double? Or was I hallucinating?"

"Yes, it was Devlin. He has no double, and both your visual acuity and your sanity are quite intact."

"Well, what the devil was he up to?"

"He was up to nothing less than assassination. The very crime we so accurately anticipated."

"But, but he—"

"To begin with he was not–and is not–Cromwell Devlin."

"Not Devlin! The devil you say. Not Devlin. Who then, pray tell, was–is–he?"

Holmes drew the razor carefully across his Adam's apple. I drew myself up and tentatively lowered my feet to the floor. The injured leg throbbed mercilessly.

"He, my dear Watson, was and is Patrick the Piper."

"Patrick the Piper," I exclaimed, dumbfounded.

"Patrick the Piper. None other. His real identity eludes us, but Steele has taken his fingerprints and, with patience, Sir Francis's ingenious method of classification[15] will reveal his real identity."

"Good heavens, Holmes. How long have you—? Are you sure? How can you—?"

Holmes laughed softly at my consternation.

"How long have I known? Well, to be truthful, since Montreal."

"Since Montreal," I shouted. I confess that my normal British reserve was wearing thin. I lowered my voice self-consciously. "Holmes, how could it be? And why did I not have an inkling of this?"

Holmes rinsed the remaining flecks of soap from his neck and carefully proceeded to dry his razor.

---

[15] An apparent reference to Sir Francis Galton who, with Juan Vucetitch, developed a practical system for matching fingerprints in 1891.

"It was better that you continued to take our associate at face value. A clever rogue such as he would quickly detect the slightest alteration in our approach. Your faith and confidence kept him somewhat less cautious—at any rate, more confident in the success of his imposture."

"But surely, Holmes, am I so gullible?"

"You are a man with immense trust in your fellow man, and that is a commendable quality in anyone," Holmes replied, placing his razor carefully into its green velvet bag.

"You see, Watson, there were an assortment of minor clues, minor discrepancies, which, taken together, added up to treachery." He laughed disarmingly.

"To begin with, you must have observed the apparently nervous drumming of Devlin's fingers—or more precisely, the little finger of his right hand—during moments of discussion or contemplation."

"Yes, as you mention it, he did frequently rap, as you say. A most annoying habit, I might add," I recalled.

"Most dedicated performers upon the Great Highland Bagpipe develop the unconscious habit of exercising the little finger for the doubling known as a birl," Holmes continued. "Indeed, the habit often identifies one piper to another as Coll did of Rory—'You have the skill of the pipes; I know by the drum of your fingers on the horn spoon.' And although I prefer the violin to the bagpipe, I readily recognized this peculiarity in our acquaintance."

The esoteric trivia that Holmes displayed never failed to amaze me, even after all these years.

The angular chin and sparsely fleshed cheeks of my colleague were even more pronounced than usual, evidence of the rigours of the recent journey to this remote outpost. "Furthermore, Watson, no ardent Ulsterite would refer to his home as Derry. That is a republican quirk, as you well know."

"You are right, absolutely right. I do now recall that Devlin talked of Derry, not Londonderry. That is a fact."

"Then, too, if you will recall, when we visited the Sailor's Church in Montreal, this man, who presumably was an unbending foe of the

Roman faith, could scarcely enter the sanctuary without attending to the proper rituals of devotion."

"Again, now that you mention it, he did seem strangely at home there."

"Rare would be the Orangeman who would betray the awe that this man calling himself Cromwell Devlin struggled to suppress."

Everything Holmes pointed out was perfectly true. It was so simple.

"And is that why you took the sudden notion of visiting that place?" I asked.

"Indeed it was. Something was not quite right, Watson. It was but a simple experiment, designed to test nothing more than a hunch," he continued. "Besides, I did genuinely wish to see the well-known landmark."

"But where was, or is, the real Cromwell Devlin—our contact?"

"I'm afraid he is dead," replied Holmes sadly.

"Then Devlin, or rather Patrick the Piper, had already killed him and disposed of him before ever we met the villain at the Montreal pier."

"No. It would appear that poor Devlin was indeed waylaid by thugs in the employ of those enemies of Britain in Montreal, Gaelic or Gallic, but that, in some fashion, he escaped."

"How can you possibly know that?" I demanded. It seemed to me impossible that Holmes could have evidence for this assertion. How could he know?

Holmes had now completed his preparations for the day. Setting aside his toiletries, he stepped to the window and looked out into the street below with its stray dogs, assorted horses and wagons, and its colourful and varied array of humanity presenting a picture at once shabby and magnificent. Holmes always enjoyed these moments in a case—the deliberate unfolding, leaf by logical leaf, of the fragile and mysterious record. I waited.

"I know that for the very simple reason that I saw him die before our hotel door in Winnipeg."

I was aghast. The recollection of that pitiful scene had never retreated far from my consciousness.

"That was Devlin?" I exclaimed. "How do you know it was Devlin?"

"You remember the blood?"

"How could one forget? Even a surgeon can be moved by the wretched gore of a butchery like that."

"You remember the blood on the wall?"

"Yes, yes. The handprint."

"Not a pleasant sight," said Holmes.

"Indeed not."

"But too clear and too deliberate to be only the flailing of a man in the paroxysms of his death agony."

"Well, perhaps. I'm not certain, Holmes. Dying men may be quite unpredictable."

"But a dying man does not draw his hand deliberately through his wound and stretch across the corridor and, with a supreme effort, place his hand carefully and precisely upon the wall, expending his last measure of energy–resigning himself then to death in the knowledge that he has done all it is humanly possible to do in order to convey the warning." "Good heavens, Holmes, what message? What warning? There was no attempt at a scrawled message–just a simple handprint. Why?"

"Not a simple handprint, but a courageous and ingenious effort by a dying man to convey a crucial message."

"The Red Hand–tribal emblem of the famed high king of ancient Ireland," I murmured.

The legend began to return to me from the dark recesses of schoolboy memory.

"And, of course, the Red Hand has become the symbol of the Ulsterite cause in these days of Ireland's agony," Holmes concluded.

"Remarkable," I confessed. My admiration was unbounded. His revelations burst like shafts of sunlight upon a misty moor. The landscape of our mission seemed to emerge with some clarity for the first time. Yet there were still obscure ravines and shadowed vales in my understanding.

"What of the lost reservations aboard the *Oceana*? Was there more than coincidence in that? And what about that fellow calling himself Paget–the fraudulent cleric?" The questions flooded forth.

"I do believe that Moriarity has lent his evil hands at last to the cause of treason. And although I cannot prove that our passage aboard that vessel was thwarted at his command, I feel it intuitively. Likely, 'the Piper' had passage on it, and those privy to the plot felt it best to avoid any chance encounter and potential exposure."

"A mark of the enemy's respect for your powers of observation," I injected.

"A clever adversary never underestimates the capacity of his foe."

Holmes returned his gaze to the window. Beyond him, the green expanse of the mountainside was momentarily bathed in brilliant Yukon sunshine.

"And with respect to the impostor who posed as the clergyman, I suspect he was only trying to get a ministerial discount. Finding Moriarity's hand in that suggests one may overestimate an adversary as well as underestimating him," Holmes chuckled. "There are times when a seemingly innocuous couple is just that—an innocuous couple. When one deals with the devious forms of evil we are accustomed to, it is easy to find deception where it does not exist."

"Well, if I may ask, Holmes, what was the connection between the Arctic and Puget Sound Cavalry and the Irish blackguards who contacted them when the *President Polk* was under repair?"

"A pair of Fenians whose organization's goals seemed to mesh nicely with the territorial ambitions of that band of Yanks. It was an effort at coordination, but a Johnny-come-lately troop of land grabbers likely had little understanding of the mix of malevolence and romance that drives Hibernian rabble-rousers, whose quarrel with Britannia is centuries older and more profound than was ever that between London and her thirteen colonies."

Holmes stepped to the crude wooden bureau, carefully replaced his razor in its pouch, and proceeded to organize his kit. I rose somewhat unsteadily from the bed and stepped to the window. Leaning on the sill, I looked into the street below. So far from civilization, so far from London and Westminster, and yet, as the Union Jack fluttered from the crude pole on the post office across the street, a keen sense of satisfaction gripped me.

"The Crown still prevails, and British justice continues the order of the day, Holmes. Thanks to you."

Holmes offered a modest demurrer, but the satisfaction on his face was clear.

Sam Steele paid us a courtesy call the following day as we prepared to take our leave of this wilderness metropolis. His words of commendation certainly seemed genuine.

"I should not be surprised if a knighthood will be in the offing for you, Mr Holmes," he said with no hint of false flattery.

The same thought had crossed my mind.

"A most generous compliment, Superintendent. But these events must remain private. Our reward is the knowledge that the Yukon will remain firmly within the Empire. At least at this point, American expansionism has been successfully thwarted."

"I will heartily second that," said I.

Steele clearly shared our satisfaction. A colonial he might be, but few Englishmen could surpass him in ability and competence.

"And what are your plans, now that the high tide of the great Yukon rush seems about to ebb?" asked Holmes, putting a final knot in the drawstring of the only large duffel he planned to take back with him on the long but infinitely easier trip by steamboat to the mouth of the Yukon River.

"Well, Mr Holmes, I will tell you that I have a strong inkling that those cursed Boer farmers are going to start something that Her Imperial Majesty will have to attend to very soon. And if war does come, I will raise a regiment of horse to see that Canada does its share for the cause."

"A noble sentiment," I said warmly. The steamboat at the landing gave a piercing blast of its whistle. Dense black smoke belched from its stack. It was time to go.

Steele accompanied us to the embankment—the same cluttered noisy disarray that had greeted us on our arrival now giving us a farewell. Warm handshakes and appropriate words completed, Holmes and I boarded the vessel. Finding a few crowded inches along the railing, we waved a final greeting to the imposing figure in his scarlet uniform, leather polished and brass burnished. Around him stood as varied an assortment of humanity as can be imagined: Eskimos, half-breeds, ragged Argonauts and chasers of dreams, confidence men, derelicts, young men of character, loose women, the hard-working and the lazy, the generous and the selfish. No bazaar in Lahore ever provided a more colourful scene. Dawson City faded in the distance, and the strong primordial current of the Yukon carried us around the bend.

"There is still one unanswered question here in the Yukon," Holmes said thoughtfully as he turned from the railing.

"And what is that?" I asked.

"Where will the boundary between British territory and that of the Yankee Republic finally be established?"

"An interesting question," I agreed, recalling the tattered remnants of the Union Jack atop the pass and remembering the gallant effort of the Canadian lads to give it its rightful place atop the Skagway Post Office.

"You know, Watson, these Canadians are a youthful and proud people. They have much to contribute to the Empire."

"I am sure of that. I've heard them claim the coming century as theirs. It may be so." I asserted.

"And it may well be that the Old Country, as they call it, will have difficult decisions to make with regard to the Dominion and its republican neighbour to the south."

"How is that?" I asked.

"The Canadian-American Joint Commission shows little ability to solve its own problems. You may recall it's in adjournment now, and my guess is it will never reassemble."

"And so?"

"And so England shall become involved. And in the final analysis, we will choose American goodwill over Canadian ambitions."

"You mean to say an Englishman might side with the Yanks against the wishes and interests of loyal British subjects?"

"That is precisely what I mean, my dear Watson."

"Impossible. Unthinkable. Never will it happen."

A blast of the steamboat whistle shattered the profound silence of this mighty wilderness. The strong current of this mighty stream carried our vessel forward in the opalescent dusk of this strange land of the midnight sun.

EPILOGUE BY THE EDITOR

By the time Holmes and Watson reached the Klondike, the gold rush had already passed its peak. Argonauts had already begun to pursue their dreams of gold in other places such as Nome, and as far away as Australia. After lengthy negotiations, the Alaskan Boundary dispute was settled in 1903. In these negotiations, the sole English member of the six-member commission, Lord Alverstone, voted with the three Americans—and against the two Canadians—making the vote in favour of the American position four to two. Great power politics did outweigh considerations of British imperial sentiment. Canadians were chagrined, to say the least. Great Britain and the United States, at the time, had significant diplomatic interests in common that overrode the ideals of imperial accord that Joseph Chamberlain was then seeking to promote. Skagway, of course, was confirmed as American territory, as it remains today.

Samuel Steele's role as custodian of law and order became less pressing as the number of miners and other adventurers declined, and shortly, he left the Yukon to found the Lord Strathcona Horse. This famed regiment participated on behalf of Canada in the Boer War, which broke out in South Africa shortly after Holmes and Watson returned to Baker Street. Again Holmes, according to Watson's account, seems to have quite accurately anticipated that unfortunate event.